REVERSED

A NOVEL BY GINA WEST

The beautiful ones always smash the picture...

PUBLISHER'S NOTE:
This book is a work of fiction. Names, characters, businesses,
Organizations, places, events and incidents are the product of the
Author's imagination or are used fictionally. Any resemblance of
Actual persons, living or dead, events, or locales are entirely coin-
cidental.

Library of Congress Control Number: 2011908156
ISBN 10: 0982391366
ISBN 13: 978-0982391365
Cover Design: Davida Baldwin www.oddballdsgn.com
Editor: Advanced Editorial Services
Graphics: Davida Baldwin
www.thecartelpublications.com
First Edition

Printed in the United States of America

CHECK OUT OTHER TITLES BY THE CARTEL PUBLICATIONS

WWW.THECARTELPUBLICATIONS.COM

What's Up Fam!!

Wow, I just want to start off this letter stating I Love Ya'll! You are the reason The Cartel Publications still holds strong in the industry and are expanding. Also, if you are having a hard time getting our books, we just got our van beautifully wrapped. So we will be hitting the road this summer. Hit us up on Facebook and Twitter and tell us where you are so we can come see you with our books on deck!

Now on to the book in hand, "Reversed" is the story of that old saying, "be careful what you wish for because you just might get it." Sometimes being happy with the person you are truly needs to be enough. Especially when wishing for someone else's life may look cool on the outside, but once you are in their shoes, shit ain't always sweet!

Aight ya'll in keeping with tradition, with every novel you all know by now we shine the spotlight on an author who is either a vet or a new comer making their way in this literary world. In this novel, we recognize:

"KiKi Swinson"

KiKi Swinson is the author of the "Wifey" series. She has also penned other novels such as, "Candy Shop", "Still Candy Shopping", "Notorious", "A Sticky Situation"and "Playing Dirty". KiKi has been in the game grinding for years and The Cartel Publications recognizes and appreciates her hustle. Go grab her titles if you not up on 'em.

On that note Fam, I'ma leave ya'll to it! Be on the lookout for our next big releases, "Raunchy 2: Mad's Love" by the beautiful and talented, T. Styles. Also, "Larceny 2: The Gift & The Curse" by my big homie Jason Poole!

Be easy!

Charisse "C. Wash" Washington
VP, The Cartel Publications

www.thecartelpublications.com
www.twitter.com/cartelbooks
www.facebook.com/publishercharissewashington
www.myspace.com/thecartelpublications
www.facebook.com/cartelcafeandbooksstore

DEDICATION

I dedicate this to people who are confident enough to
live their own lives.

Dumb

(THE SUMMER OF 2000)

I could smell the difference between them, but I still stayed. If I woulda left, he probably wouldn't be with me no more. Since he's my first boyfriend, I didn't want that to happen. So I played dumb and stayed on my knees in the dark Laundromat pretending as if I couldn't tell the difference between my boyfriend's dick and his two friends.

Knowing the difference was really easy though. Jamal's jeans smelled like coconut and fried chicken, since we were at my house earlier and that's what my mom cooked. While one of his friends smelled like sex, like he had been fucking some nasty girl a few minutes earlier. The last one smelled like soap...and I appreciated that. I had to appreciate something to make me not leave this stinky place. I told myself anybody woulda did what I was doing for their boyfriend. You know...by suckin' his friends off too. I hoped it was true, even though I was sure that it wasn't.

1

My mouth was getting sore from holding it open so long and my throat felt clumpy having swallowed Jamal and the smelly one's cum. Although I wanted so badly to go home, the clean smellin' one was taking too long to bust. I even moaned a little, like I enjoyed it, hopin' he would hurry up. But still, he took his time all the while making my *job* harder. It was like he was trying to stretch shit out on purpose…for what I don't know.

With all the pain I was in, I continued to let my boyfriend use me in the darkness for him and his friends' amusement. It's so dark that I couldn't see my hands in front of my face if I tried. All I could do was smell their stinky bodies mixed with the rusty water odor from the broken pipes in the basement. Between the smell and the pain I was in from my mouth being sore and my knees pressing against the cold concrete floor, I didn't know if I was *coming* or going. But I wished he did, quick!

The moment Jamal asked me to give him head in the Laundromat of his dirty apartment building in the projects he lived in and demanded that the lights stay out, I knew something was up. We were just at my house and my mother and father would not have been back home for another hour. So why leave? He was so pressed to do it in his building! Jamal always tried to impress his friends. It wasn't enough that he enjoyed what we did in *private*; he had to use me in *public*. When we entered the Laundromat's door and I heard footsteps moving silently in the darkness, my intuition was confirmed. We were not alone.

When we first entered the basement and I finished sucking him off he said, "Give me a sec. I want you to do it again."

That was his way of buying time for them to switch. One by one they got in front of me and placed their limp things in my mouth. Some people would say I'm dumb and I can't say that I'm not. All I knew was that I had two choices. Say no and lose my boyfriend or say yes and lose my reputation. Between the two, losing my rep' was a chance I was willing to take but losing my boyfriend was out of the question.

"Thanks, Kiante," Jamal whispered from the left while his friend zippened his pants in front of me. Tears sprung to my eyes. The least he coulda did was pretended I just finished doin' him and not his friend by standing in front of me instead of yelling across the room. "Stay right here until I leave." He continued.

"Why?" I asked in the direction of his voice.

This total darkness shit was startin' to scare me a little and for a moment, I wondered what his friends thought of me. My question was answered when I heard them snicker. My face was flushed with my own embarrassment. Couldn't they at least pretend they weren't in the basement?

"Did I do it right, Jamal?"

"Hmm hmm."

"You sure?"

"Hmm hmm."

"I love you, Jamal."

"Hmm Hmm," he repeated.

I wanted him to believe that *I believed* that I was clueless of his actions and how he betrayed our bond. "Do you love me back?"

"Stop askin' questions and don't come upstairs for five minutes! I don't want nobody to know we were in here," his voice sounded irritated and low.

"Okay." I responded letting him off easy not wanting him to carry me in front of his friends any more.

Lucia, my best friend's sister, told me to leave Jamal alone a long time ago. I paid her no attention because Lucia was the kind of girl who got anybody she wanted. Pretty couldn't even be used to describe her. Even Jamal wanted her at first but after she shot him down, due to liking older boys, he pursued me instead. They all pursued me *instead.*

As their feet scurried up the stairs, I remained on my knees with my back faced the door. When the door closed and I was alone in the silence and darkness again, I stood up, brushed off my knees and inhaled my own shame. It stunk more than anything I'd ever done in all my life. My only hope was that after this, Jamal would still want me.

After all, I did what no other girl probably would have, pleased him and his friends at the same time.

After I took the walk of shame from the basement, I glanced down at the grey stairs. There was an empty Doritos chip bag and some other trash scattered on the steps. For some reason, the red bag stood out. I thought about how at one point, someone wanted the bag and when its contents were gone, they threw it away, just like me.

When I reached the top step and pushed the steel green door open, the bright spring sun blinded me. I briefly looked upon the business of Washington D.C. and the projects called Tyland Towers. Everybody was going about life doing regular shit. For a second I didn't see Jamal or his friends but when I turned my head to the left, they were there. It angered me that Jamal didn't bother to tell them to get lost, to keep in line with the trick he thought he played on me. When it dawned on me who was next to him, I threw up right there.

"What the fuck?!" Jamal yelled out as some of the contents of my stomach, which included him and his friend's semen, got on his shoes. "What the fuck are you doing?"

"Nothin'," I said holding onto the rail as the other two jumped up and away from me, not wanting to get anything else I was getting ready to bring up on them. "I just don't feel well."

"Well watch out!" Jamal continued.

As I wiped my mouth with the back of my hand, I glanced up at who was with him. It was funky Chris and Raheem from around the way.

Now Chris *never* took a bath because he always wanted to go outside. He swore if he didn't spend every waking minute outside he'd miss somethin'. No matter how nasty, he still believed he was the shit because he wore designer clothes. But no matter what brand name clothes he wore he *still* looked dumpy, like the clothes weren't his or somethin'. Like right now he was wearing a pair of Diesel jeans, a white t-shirt and a pair of all white and green Stan Smith Adidas tennis shoes. Anybody else rocking somethin' like that looked clean, but he looked dirty. His hair stayed in a bushy ponytail that sat on the top of his head and his light skin always looked bruised or beaten. People said he was abused by the next door neighbor his mother left him with while she ran the streets, but he was still bad. Maybe he wasn't gettin' beat enough.

I knew he didn't even like me because he told Jamal my lips were too big and then Jamal told me what he said. Humph! I see he ain't waste no time getting in line to get his dick sucked. My tongue was probably the first thing that washed his dick all day! Yuck!

"You alright, Kiante!" Chris asked me like he cared about how I felt. He almost sounded like he was ashamed about his part in all of this.

Jamal looked at him and shot a look because speaking to me was unusual. Me and Chris could be standing right next to each other in the hallway at school and either he'd ignore me or yell out something like, *"Yo, you got some big ass lips!"*

"I'm alright, Chris," I said never looking into his eyes. "Thanks."

"You sure?" Raheem followed as he tilted his head to the left. "Cuz you still looked fucked up."

"Yes I am," I responded dryly. "I just wanna go home that's all."

Raheem was known throughout Ballou High School in Southeast as *the* rapist. If a girl didn't give him what he wanted he wouldn't trip. He'd just take it from her later. Everybody kept sayin' he was too handsome to take anything but I don't think it was about that with him. My mom's is going to school for psychology and she says most rapists like to take *control* and that the sex is almost never their motive.

As much as I couldn't stand him, Raheem stayed fresh. I figured he must've been the clean one I smelled earlier. Raheem was always clean and took pride in his appearance and his clothes. His style was similar to Jamal's and Chris' meaning that less was more. None of them liked a whole bunch of patterns and flashy logo designs on their clothes, even if it was name brand. It was always crisp Hanes t-shirts, fresh jeans and new kicks. Raheem kept his hair in neat cornrows and rocked a new pair of Jordan's every time I saw him. The small mole under his right eye against his dark brown skin made him appear harmless even though the opposite was true.

After Chris and Raheem spoke, the silence was uncomfortable. It only lasted for thirty seconds, but it felt like a lifetime because the person I was waiting to say something remained silent. I couldn't help but wonder if he dumped me already.

"Look, Kiante," he said looking at Victor, the neighborhood drug dealer's son, rough up some kid in the grass. "I ain't goin' back to the house wit' you tonight." His eyes remained on Victor, even after he just broke my heart.

"Why?" My nose stung with that sensation which always let me know that I was on the verge of crying. I was trying to pull myself together but the more I tried, the harder it became to do.

"Cuz." He finally said as he looked at me and then away again.

"Cuz what, Jamal?" *Shit! Give me something!* Here I was waiting for him to come up with an excuse to why he was carrying me and he didn't even think enough of me to have an answer ready. I'm sure he knew he wasn't going back with me the moment I finished with them in the basement.

As if a light bulb went off in his head he said, "I'm goin' over Jodi's with Chris and Rah! Jodi got that new NBA2K game." The moment he

8

lied Chris and Raheem snickered under their breath and I felt like slappin' the livin' shit out of all of them.

"Okay, Jamal." My voice was low. I kept it that way so he couldn't tell I was already crying. You can do that you know. Cry inside so that nobody knows, even if they're standing right in front of you. "Can you call me later?"

"Maybe…maybe not."

"What's up wit' all of this, Jamal? Did I do something wrong?"

"You tell me." He responded back.

I hadn't expected him to confront me about what I did just moments earlier but with the cold shoulder he was giving, I realized I was wrong.

"Listen," he started. "I just want to be wit' my boys right now. I'll call you if I get a chance. Cool?"

"Yeah…" I responded. "It's cool."

As I walked down the stairs and past Victor and his friends, I put fire in my steps so I could make it to my car without crying my eyes out in front of them. How could I be so stupid?! I shoulda known that he wouldn't want me if I did that shit! But what was I to do, tell him I knew what he was doin' by sneakin' them in there, slap him in the face and leave? I couldn't do that shit! If I did, then that woulda brought attention to the reason for him doin' it in the first place. I didn't want to be faced with the fact that he didn't want to be with me anyway, that's why he tricked me off to his friends. Instead, I made myself believe he did it because he wanted his friends to know what they were missin' out on by not being with me. Now I realized that was not the case.

With the weight of the embarrassment I felt heavy on my shoulders; I sat in my green Kia Sephia and pounded the steering wheel giving myself a premature headache. The voice of reason my mother placed in my head about respecting myself was getting on my damn nerves. It kept telling me that what I just did would forever change who I was inside…and I wanted it to stop talking to me. I didn't need its opinion! I needed and wanted Jamal!

Unlike my friends Lucia and Marissa, I didn't come from the projects or a broken home. My mother and father were still together and living in a small little house in Oxon Hill Maryland. You're probably wondering why I go to Ballou in D.C. since I live in Maryland. *Well*, it was because I'm an only child and my mother and father sometimes give me what I want, even when I don't deserve it. They call themselves helping me out with my social crisis.

That's why they bought me the car and allowed me to use Lucia and Marissa's address, to go to the same school they were in. Their only request was that I maintain a 3.0 grade point average and I blew that out the water. My grades were never a problem, but my personal life was. As hard as I tried, I could never really fit in so my family did what they could to help me with this. It wasn't easy considering my mother was in her last year at John Hopkins University to become a psychologist and my father was trying to get his construction business off the ground. Still, they did whatever they could for me including buying me *some* of the things I thought would increase my status at school. But now I'm starting to wonder how much my quest for popularity will really cost me.

DADDY NEVER DID IT
KIANTE

I sat in my car outside of Lucia and Marissa's building. I couldn't believe how pretty Lucia's shiny royal blue Acura Integra was. Hempay, her boyfriend really laced her up. Lucia was so pretty that any dude would've been dying to do what Hempay wouldn't. But since he loved her more than anything, she stayed by his side.

Lucia looked like a young J-Lo, *body* included. To be honest Lucia and Marissa were both beautiful and their full-bred Puerto Rican heritage helped. Don't get me wrong I loved being black but I told them all the time that if I *had* to choose another race, it would definitely be Latino. Besides, Latino people are just like us. I call them light-skinned niggas. The only difference is, their food is a bit spicier.

I adjusted the mirror to look at my face. Look at me. I'm a skinny, dark-skin girl with a body that goes straight up and down. I ain't got no ass, no titties and no hips. The one thing I do have a lot of, I don't want and that's big lips. My daddy told me that when I'm older, I'll learn to appreciate them. I'm still waiting on that day.

REVERSED

I removed the baby-wipes from the glove compartment of my Kia and wiped them (Jamal, Chris and Raheem) from my mouth. I was so caught into my shame that I forgot to do it. I searched my glove compartment for a Lifesaver or a piece of gum but couldn't find anything. I'll ask Marissa for a tooth brush when I get in her house since her mother always bought everything in bulk. She could never buy just one of anything. She swore there was no need cuz stuff was cheaper the more you bought. I wonder if she was thinking the same thing when she bought six gallons of milk because they were fifteen percent off, only to throw four of them in trash because they went spoiled. Lucia and Marissa were happy when Mamma Maria threw them away because before that, they had to drink milk morning, noon and night just to get rid of it.

Getting out of my car I tried to walk with my head up. With each step I took, I was starting to see that it was harder to do. It was a good thing the door leading to their building was right next to where we parked our cars, in the alley. I didn't feel like walking around front and past all of that bullshit on the steps that goes on.

I could hear Lucia and Marissa fighting the moment I got to their door. They weren't close like sisters should be, they were far from it. Lucia had a thing for carrying both of us when she was around her friends at school and only gave us the time of day when we were at home. Even then, she walked with a chip on her shoulders and her head up in the air.

"Who is it?!" Lucia yelled.

"It's me, Lucia. Open the door."

"Hey, girl!" She responded as if she was happy to see me. I loved how she could wear her hair in a ponytail and it still looked cute. I had to go to the hair salon every weekend if I wanted my hair to look decent. My girl Marissa although she didn't have to, went to the hair salon with me every time. "Come in!"

As I looked her up and down I was a bit jealous. She looked real cute in her red valor short set by J-Lo. Her tiny waist, big butt and perfect legs made my skinny ones look like pencils. *Damn*! Why couldn't I be blessed with a body like hers?

As I walked in the house and toward Marissa's room, I saw their mother Maria in the kitchen doin' what she did best…cooking. I had to speak to her before I got up with Marissa. Maria is *the* coolest mother in the world. You can tell that from the moment she could walk, she was raised around us because she was definitely hip. Marissa and Maria fit the same sizes so Marissa stayed stealing her mother's clothes and wearing them to school. I couldn't blame her, because if my mom wore the labels like Maria, I would, too.

But the thing I liked about her the most, was her giving spirit, and the only thing I didn't care for was her man. J.D was a 23-year old punk who would beat her once a month for no reason. Her features use to be as pretty and as vibrant as her daughters, before the abuse she was receiving started to set in. Don't get me wrong, Maria could still get down with the best of them. She wasn't no slouch, just not as cute as she could be. While I'm looking at her now, I could see a recent bruise under her eye. I didn't force her to remember it by staring at it. I pretended like she did, that it wasn't there.

"Kiante!" She smiled when she saw me walk in the kitchen stretching her arms out to me. "Why didn't you tell me you were coming, mija?" I loved the way she called me mija, which was Spanish slang for "my daughter". It really made me feel part of the family. Maria always mixed Spanish words and phrases into her English a *little* because she was around her mother who only knew Spanish for *half* of her life. "I coulda' packed you a bag to take home to your mamma. I have so many stuff I tryin' to get reed of."

Sitting at the table I saw the spread she had on the stove. My nose anticipated what everything tasted like. She had fried chicken, yellow rice with gravy, collard greens and buttered biscuits in the oven. Mamma Maria grabbed a white porcelain plate out of the wooden cabinet and dished up a health serving. My mouth watered when she placed it in front of me, it made a clinking noise against the table. If you came over to Mamma Maria's you were bound to get something to eat every time.

"No, Mamma Maria," I laughed. "I'm not hungry." I lied because I knew she would persist, plus my mother told me bein' greedy was rude.

"Nonsceeense!" She responded waving her hand in front of me. "You as skinny as my arm." She was right. "My food will make you theek. Just like me," she smiled before pointing in my direction and slapping herself on her butt. "Soy caliente!"

"Yes you are, Mamma Maria!" I laughed. "You are hot!"

Seconds later Lucia came in the kitchen kissed her mother and said, "Okay, mamma, Hempay is here to pick me up. You want anything while we're out?" When Lucia started digging in the pots with her fingers without washing her hands, I was disgusted. It almost ruined my appetite. That's some nasty shit! Although Maria taste tested the food...she was allowed, she was the cook but Lucia wasn't. But after I tasted my piece of chicken I knew there was no way on *earf* I was throwing mine away.

"You tell me son-in-law I said come in here and bring to me my hug!" Mamma Maria liked Hempay, we all did. He was the kinda nigga you just liked. At 6 foot 2 inches tall, he demanded your attention the moment he walked in the room. As handsome as he was, you gave it to him. He had the

darkest skin with the prettiest soft hair I'd ever
seen. He usually kept it braided but I loved it the
most when he pulled it back into a ponytail, because he was in between getting his hair braided.
"Go on, Lucia! I want to see him."

"Okay, mamma! Dang!" Lucia sashayed to
the door her ponytail swaying from left to right.
"Hem! Come here, baby. Mami wants to see you." I
felt a tinge of jealousy but I pushed it aside. I like
Lucia, so much that I wanted to be like her.

The moment he came through the door, he
flashed a smile so bright at Maria, I had to turn
away. Playing with my food I tried to pretend this
17 year old body didn't long to be on top of his. His
diamond embedded watch glistened perfectly up
against his skin. Listen to me! Glistened?! I sound
like I've been reading too many romance novels.

"Hey, Ms. Alvarez!" His voice was deep
and raspy, like somewhere along the line he ditched
the 17 year old boy and became a man. "Sorry I
ain't come in here. We on our way to the movies."

"I ain't seen you in I don know how long."
She stroked his face and looked into his eyes. I
wondered what she was thinking and if she knew
like she always said that he would someday be her
son-in-law.

"This food smellin' good," he responded,
smile still on his face as he lifted up the tops on the
stove.

"Taste!" She grinned placing a piece of chicken in his mouth. His arms wrapped around her waist and for a second I wondered if she got aroused by the way he was holding her. Shit, any woman with a thing for men had to unless they were gay. Don't get me wrong, I know it was *perfectly* innocent but Hempay had a thing with flirting that was sexy. "You like, don't you?" Maria said nodding her head. Food was nothing but an aphrodisiac.

His face lit up as he savored Mamma Maria's cooking'. I didn't blame him. There ain't but one other woman on the face of this earth that can cook betta than her and that's my mamma.

"Ms. Alzarez," he smiled giving her that flirtatious grin and a wink. "Why don't we ditch your daughter and them and get married."

"Cut it out, Hempay!" She giggled giving him a tap on the shoulder with her kitchen towel. "You my daughter's future husband!"

"What I want with that when I can have the creator?" He laughed looking at Lucia. She stuck her tongue out and shook her head to all of their carrying on. "With cookin' like this I'd be in heaven."

He was laying it on thick and I could see she was eating every bit of it up. By the time he finished with her, she wouldn't want nothing to eat cuz she'd be full. When she laughed a bit harder and the hair covering the bruise on her face was revealed, all playin' ceased. Hempay's beautiful dark skin turned red. I would not have been surprised if he punched a whole in the wall.

"What happened to your face?" He was questioning Lucia's mother as if he were her man.

"Notheen!" she said as she walked away from him and toward the refrigerator. She procrastinated with the door open like she was looking for something. But I knew what she was looking for because I tried to find it earlier, after I left Jamal and his friends. She was lookin' for her pride. "You kids go along now. I got theengs to do here."

Hempay walked up behind her as Lucia called his name. She knew what her mother was trying to do, avoid having a discussion about J.D's punk ass hitting her.

"Come on, Hempay! We gonna be late for the movie," she yelled holding the door open.

He shot her a look so mean, that all she could do was calm down and close the door. Hempay already stepped to J.D and told him not to hit his girl's mother, but apparently he wasn't listening.

"Mamma, I'ma tell you again, and listen to me cuz I ain't playin' no more." His hands moved like a rapper when he was tryin' to show he was serious. Mamma Maria turned around looked at his Timbs instead of his face. "If he put his hands on you again, I'ma break his jaw." He gently lifted her chin forcing her to look into his eyes. "You hear me right?"

"*Si*," she breathed out. "Yes, I hear you."

With that he walked away from her and noticed me sitting at the table. "Hey pretty, I ain't know you were here." His eyes sparkled like I was his lil sista or something. It always made me feel good.

He was the only man besides my father who called me pretty every time he saw me. I think he's just bein' nice, but I like it anyway. Unlike his girl, he was the same way *every* time I saw him, even at Ballou. We were all in our last year at school and I noticed that lately he didn't like guys looking at me. Sometimes he acted like my father. What I also liked about Hempay besides everything was that he was the only hustler who was serious about school, and that made him even sexier.

"Hey, Hempay!" My eyes remained on my food. I can't look at him because he might see what I really feel about him. "Where ya'll goin'?"

"Out!" Lucia responded grabbing her man.

"I'll see you at school tomorrow," he smiled as he was hauled off. "Lada."

As they walked out the door, J.D, walked in. "What up, man?" His hands gestured for Hempay to give him some dap. Hempay looked in his eyes, gritted and walked off with Lucia. Closing the door, he glanced over me and grabbed Mamma Maria by the hair. "You tellin' that nigga my bizness again?!"

"No, J.D!" Her hands shaking and in front of her face as if they could shield her from whatever he was getting ready to bring.

I was stunned, I knew J.D beat Mamma Maria but I never thought he'd do it in front of me. His ashy black hands gripped her thick black hair like he was tryin' to squeeze blood out of it. All I wanted him to do was to let her go. But me being the punk I was remained seated. I never saw anything like this before. Why a man gotta hit a woman? All I saw my father ever do to my mother was love her.

The fright on Mamma Maria's face was horrifying! She looked like Death and the Devil were coming to take her away and she wasn't ready. When he came across her face with a closed fist, and knocked her to the floor, I screamed. I didn't know if this fool was gonna start hitting me next or what. My screams startled him and he knocked over the pot of chicken on the counter and to the floor. As I sat in terror too scared to move, Marissa crept in and pulled me back to her room. If she didn't come get me, I ain't know how I was gonna make it.

"Why your mother stay with J.D?"

"I don't know, Kiante...and I don't wanna talk about it either." It pissed me off that Mamma Maria was being pimped slapped in the kitchen while Marissa browsed through her book collection as if nothing happened. "But did you read this yet?"

She had some book in her hand but I wasn't focusing on it. Instead I stared at this girl like she was trippin' because she was. She actually didn't give a fuck that a 23 year old punk was beating her forty somethin' year old mother like it was nothing. We could still hear her cries now.

"Do you care that J.D is whooping your mother's ass for no reason? Or is it just me?"

She plopped down on the bed beside me with the book in hand. I still don't know which one it was nor did I care. I was waiting on Marissa to suggest we call the police or somethin', instead of sitting here and doing nothing. Instead she said, "J.D's cool. He'll stop in a minute."

"He'll stop in a minute? Fuck are you talkin' 'bout, Marissa? You can't be serious."

She stood up and placed the book back on the shelf my father made for her last year. They wasn't supposed to be building shit in this apartment, but in the projects everybody did what they wanted to anyway. I finally glanced at the book she placed back and made a mental note to ask her how was it later. I heard *Shyt List*, by Reign was the bomb by at least three people at school.

"My pops use to beat ma worse," she said as she walked over to the mirror and started combing her thick wavy hair that cascaded on her shoulders. "So I still rather have J.D any day and twice on Sunday."

When Marissa started talking, I finally realized what was going on. She did care. She cared a lot, but it hurt too much to talk about. Me and Marissa was more alike than I realized. I decided to let my friend off the hook so I walked to window to check on my car. Although it was only a Kia Sephia, green at that, it was still mine and niggas would still steal it. I was relieved it was still there parked next to Lucia's Acura. I guess if they had the choice they woulda stolen hers. Hempay musta drove his Range Rover to take Lucia to the movies.

"You still goin' with me to the Laundromat?" I turned around to face her.

"I don't know why you don't go to the one downstairs," she pouted. "It's cheaper and closer."

"Girl, that Laundromat is filthy," I responded going through the pictures she had scattered around on her dresser. I of all people should know how nasty it was considering I'd just sucked three dicks in one just like it earlier.

"I'll go with you but I want you to do something for me first." She had that look in her eyes that was only there when she wanted me to do something devious. I hoped she didn't want me to let her practice on kissing me again. Last time she did it, we didn't speak for three weeks. But she swore it was the only way she could learn how to kiss Dinky, her 25-year-old boyfriend, right.

"What is it?" I asked sitting on the chair in front of her pink vanity mirror and dresser set. That's the only thing about Latino people that troubled me; they loved throwing colors together that didn't match. For instance her dresser was a pink pearl color. Her bed was green and her curtains were blue. Everything in her room looked a mess with the exception of the clothes in her closet.

"I want you to tell me if you think Dinky would like something."

"Like what?"

"Something," she responded as if she was too embarrassed to show me.

"Are you gonna tell me what or do I have to drag it out of you?" I shouted.

She walked over to the bed that was directly in front of where I sat and pulled down her pants.

"What are you doin', Marissa?!" I stood straight up and ran toward the other side of the room. I don't know what she was planning but I wanted no parts of it.

"I want you to see what I got shaved on my pussy." She said it as if she had just gotten her hair fixed and she wanted my advice on how it looked.

As bad as I wanted to leave and run out of there, I was curious. What could she have shaved on her pussy that involved Dinky? Instead of walking out I said, "Show me."

She removed her pink panties and there on her pubic hairs I saw the word *Dicky*. It was razor thin but still very visible. What in the fuck was that supposed to mean? "Why would you have that shaved into your pussy?"

"Cuz," she responded shrugging her shoulders and pulling up her panties. "I wanted to prove to him that I love him. He stay thinkin' I be fuckin' with them young boys at school, so I wanted to prove to him I don't."

I walked back over to the chair because I was desperately trying to figure this all out. I mean, Marissa was a genius being as though she skipped the eleventh grade, but what she was sayin' was dumb. "Who did it?"

"This dude at the barber shop!" Again she was talking as if it was normal.

"Wait...you got that done in a public place?"

"Yep!" She walked over to her closet and started separating her clothes to go to the Laundromat with me later. "Where did he do it at?" I was full of questions, inquiring minds wanted to know.

"In the back of his shop."

"Girl you wild as shit!" I erupted into laughter knowing she'd be pissed but I couldn't help it. That shit was so funny that I almost forgot about what I did to Jamal and them, and what happened to Mamma Maria. "Which dude did you let do that, Marissa?"

"Damon." She had an attitude but she needed to. Everything about the shit was just crazy!

"Damon? Your sister's ex boyfriend?" She nodded her head yes. "You wasn't embarrassed when he did it for you?"

"Was you embarrassed when you sucked Jamal and them's dick in the Laundromat today?"

I was in shock, not because I did it but because I hadn't told her. "What you talkin' about?" My response made me guilty the moment it fell out of my mouth.

"I was on the phone with Crystal when you got here earlier. They said Jamal was tellin' everybody how he wanted to see if you would do some shit like that, and when you did, he knew he couldn't fuck wit' you no more." Now she was laughing. I wasn't.

How could he embarrass me like this? The voice of reason told me I embarrassed myself but I didn't care. There she was bagging up her dirty laundry and I felt like jumpin' right in. I was as filthy as the clothes she was putting in the bag. I felt the stinging sensation I felt earlier in my nose again. It was harder to control because now my intuitions were confirmed. He had dumped me. He didn't even do me the honor of a private dump, he dumped me in public! Crystal was the worse person to find out because she had no jaw. And when I say no jaw I don't mean physically. I meant she told so many people's business, that her mouth stayed permanently open. By the time I got back to school tomorrow, everybody would know my business and I hated it.

"Of course I told that bitch she was lying," Marissa continued feeling bad she dropped a major bomb on me. I can't lie, I was kinda happy she had my back. That's all I needed was for Crystal to tell everybody that even my best friend thought I was a freak too. "But I can tell by the way you lookin' right now that it is true. Kiante, why? Why would you do that?"

I told her everything. Well, almost everything. The last thing I needed was for my best friend to think I would purposely suck off dirty Chris and Raheem the rapist. When I finished with my side of the story, which included how they fooled me, she felt like jumping in my ride and punchin' the hell out of Jamal for trickin' me.

Trickin' me. Only if she knew that I knew exactly what I was doing.

"I'm sawwy, Kiante," she said softly giving me a hug. I wanted her to stop. Whenever a person hugged me when I was upset, it only made me cry more.

Pushing away from her I said, "I'm okay! I just know now I ain't fuckin' wit' him no more. Why the fuck would he trick me into sucking his friends dicks and then make it sound like I wanted to do it?"

"You couldn't tell for real?" Her question was doubtful and hurt a little.

"No! This the first I'm hearing about it being somebody else in there. It was dark as shit and I couldn't even see in front of me." Lies all lies, but the truth would be going with me to my grave.

"Don't worry about it girl. Maybe I'll get Dinky to fuck his weak ass up."

When she said that I realized that I still didn't know why she shaved *Dicky* in her pubic hairs so I decided to ask. Because I sure ain't feel like talkin' about being a fool no more. Talking about anything else would work for me. "So Marissa, how come you got the word *Dicky* in your hairs? Couldn't you have put somethin' else like love or somethin'?"

"*Dicky*?" Her face was shocked.

"Yeah!"

Pulling down her pants and panties again she went to the mirror. Her mouth dropped when the words read, 'YKCID'. *Dicky* backwards. "What the fuck!" She yelled.

"What's wrong?!" I wanted to know why she was so amazed.

"It was supposed to say Dinky! I'ma fuck Damon up! He play too much." She pulled up her clothes angrily while grabbing her bags and placing them next to the door.

I can't lie, the fact that it said *Dicky* instead of Dinky made me laugh again. Marissa was always funniest when she wasn't trying to be.

"That's why I'm 'bout to start fuckin' wit' Chris."

"For fuckin' what?!" My happy mood gone.

"I been likin' him, but when he came down to the shop today to get his hair cut after school, I knew how much."

"What Damon putting Dicky instead of Dinky on your pussy got to do with Chris?"

"It's like a sign."

"A sign? That ain't right, Marissa. What about what happened to me today? He tricked me into some bullshit and you don't even care."

"Yes I do, but its Jamal's fault not his. You know a nigga gonna do some shit if he can get away with it."

She was right but I still didn't think they should be together. If they kicked it, it would look even more like the joke was on me. "That boy is dirty!"

"Girl you crazy! He *stay* fresh!" she boasted.

"He *stay* dingy!" I corrected her ass.

"No he don't."

"But what about Dinky?! I like him." Dinky was real cool to hang around. He was so cool that sometimes I thought he was gay. We both did. We could sit around each other for hours and he'd fit in just like one of the girls.

"I like him too but lately he's been actin' weird."

"Weird like what?"

"He be wanting me to put my finger in his ass and all kinda shit like that. What man would want you to put your finger in his ass?"

A gay one, but I didn't tell her that. It would ruin my position for wanting her to stay with him. When I realized it was a dead issue, I left it there. Marissa's my girl but I was fucked up that she would even want to be bothered with Chris after the shit that happened earlier.

When we walked into the living room to go to the Laundromat, I didn't see J.D or Maria. I figured he was probably making up to her like most bums did when they messed up. When I stood quiet for one moment, I could hear him fucking her in the bedroom. All I can think of was today has been a fucked up day for me but at least Mamma Maria was getting fucked like she wanted.

EVEN LESS OF A REPUTATION
KIANTE

The small house I called home all my life was always cozy and recharged me every time I walked through its doors. Most of the furniture we had could easily be considered antique, but Mamma took care of everything very well. The large twill brown sofa in our living room could comfortably sit four to five people, and my daddy's favorite matching brown recliner chair had been broken in so well, that once you sat in it, it was impossible to get out. There was a glass table that sat in the middle of the living room, next to the couch that was chipped slightly on the edge due to me falling down at three years old, and bumping my eye lid on it. The small but faint scar is still there.

Our two-bedroom rambler had brown curtains throughout it, and whenever they needed to be washed, Mamma would just take them down, soak them in the tub, and hang them in the backyard to dry. On every ceiling but the one in my room hung large plants which mamma would water and talk to once a week, thinking they'd live longer if she did. Life wasn't glamorous but it was content.

I was lying comfortably on the couch with my daddy, watching *Gladiator*. My daddy always had a way of making me feel like I was safe and that everything would be okay. If only he knew what his little girl did when he wasn't around. And how not to long ago I'd given blowjobs on my knees in a dirty Laundromat for free. And if he did know, I wonder if he'd still love me the same.

"Daddy, can I borrow two hundred dollars?" I asked him as we watched television on the couch.

"Borrow?" He said in a funny tone. "You mean you actually gonna give me my money back this time?"

"Daddy," I laughed as I hit is leg. "You know what I mean."

"What you need it for, baby?"

I knew he was gonna ask me but I hadn't thought of a good enough lie yet. I had plans to give it to Jamal so that he'd stop telling people about what happened in the Laundromat. He came to me yesterday saying he needed money because I gave him something when I sucked his dick and he needed to go to the clinic to get it fixed. I had a feeling he was lying but all I needed was for him to spread that shit around. It wasn't a problem I was trying to keep.

It had been three weeks after my name became Kiante the "Whore" instead of Kiante Jenkins. Because of it, I knew my remaining days at Ballou would be hell. I started to beg my mother to transfer me to a school in Maryland but being the nerd that I was, I didn't want my grades to be messed up for college. Marissa and I had decided upon going to Howard University, in Washington D.C. together and I didn't want nothin' fuckin' that up.

When I briefly discussed with Marissa my plans for going to Oxon Hill High School in Maryland, she ranted off in her native language, although most of her words were clear. 'You're not leaving me, *puta* so don't even try it!' As mad as she was, I knew what she was really saying was that she didn't want to be left alone at the school while I didn't want to be in it.

Lately I had been thinking heavily on the new girl Jamal was messing with. She wasn't even cute. Her light-skin and bony legs were skinner than mine and her knees always appeared to knocking together. I think the real reason he got with her was because she was down with the *Strawberry Cuties,* a girl clique in our school. You weren't shit unless you were with them, hence one of my problems. Every time me and Marissa tried to get in, they'd make up some lame ass excuse to block us from getting into the group. We both knew that the *real* reason they didn't want us in was because of Lucia's hatin' ass. She couldn't stand the idea of seeing us rolling in the same circle as she did, or even worse, taking some attention off of her.

"What's on your mind, baby?" His eyes were on the TV but his mind was on me. "You wouldn't just ask me for money like that unless something really was up."

I nestled myself in his arms as I lay in front of him on the couch. For a moment I briefly inhaled the deodorant he wore and smiled. "Nothin'," I responded taking a deep breath. "I just needed to get something."

"What?" He asked. "New clothes? You got plenty of stuff in there now."

"No, daddy. I just wanted to grab a few things."

"We've always had an open relationship, Kiante."

"I know, daddy."

"Well let's keep it that way." He turned off the TV, and sat up straight on the couch, forcing me to do the same.

Once he was up, he turned around, fixed the red plaid shirt that was wrinkled because we were lying down, and looked into my eyes. Daddy was handsome. He always kept a five o'clock shadow on his face that was neatly trimmed and shaped up. His 6'4 inch, 350 pound frame seemed intimidating to some but me and mamma loved it. As I admired his eyes I smiled. He has the longest, prettiest eyelashes I ever seen on a man in my life. They softened his features, but didn't take away from the fact that he was *all* man. His voice was authoritative and deep, but his words were *always* kind and gentle.

"I am being real with you, daddy," I responded feeling guilty the moment the words fell out of my mouth. "I just really need the money that's all."

"Baby, if there's one thing I have always tried to instill in you it's that I am here for you. *Always*. You don't have to carry whatever weight that you're carrying on your own. Let me help you, honey."

Instead of answering him, I began to pluck lint off of the brown twill sofa. When I was alone, and sad, I'd lie on the couch and sniff it just because it smelled like my father's cologne and my mother's perfume.

While I focused on the meaningless task of lint picking on the couch, my father lifted my chin slightly. "You don't have to handle things on your own, Kiante." Again he repeated, "Let me help carry some of that weight for you. I'm much stronger than you realize," he continued playfully punching me in my face, forcing out a smile.

You see why I love my father? Just that quickly, he made me feel better. I only wished his words could take my problems away. All of them. I honestly believed if I told him that I sucked Jamal and his friend's off in the basement Laundromat, he'd have an answer for that too. But of course, I decided against it.

"Were you and mom popular at school?" Without waiting for an answer I grabbed his hands and studied his fingers. He had hard working blue collar hands, the kind you get from working in all types of weather for hours at a time. My daddy helped create masterpieces on the buildings he designed in the DC and Maryland area. But it was his hands, not the things that he made, that I loved, because I was sure that as long as he lived, they'd always protect me.

"Kiante," he started as if he'd known exactly what I was referring to. "Popularity is nothin' but a joke. Try not to get so caught up into that kind of stuff at school."

"It's not a joke to me, daddy," I responded releasing his hand.

"I understand you feel that inside, but it *is* a joke. The rules to being popular change all the time. The sad part about it is some people build their entire lives on trying to achieve it, only to realize later in life, that none of that shit matters."

I was listening but growing irritated at his response to my question already. I curled up my lip on the right side of my face so that he couldn't see me do it on the left. While I respect my father's opinion, he was still old. And things have changed! Look at the clothes they wore and the things we wear now. I grabbed my glass cup off the table and downed the rest of the coke and melted ice. It tasted like sugar water and I was contemplating filling it up again.

"Kiante," he said taking the cup from my hands, placing it back on the table. "You can never really achieve popularity because it's a purposeless status created by others and based on nothing."

My daddy was wise but sometimes too deep. What did that mean? A purposeless status created by others based on nothing? I didn't understand it and I really wasn't trying to hear it either. It was clear anything I said about how I felt in school, would fall on deaf ears. So I decided to keep the rest of my comments to myself.

"You don't understand what I'm saying do you?"

"Not really," I said hunching my shoulders before dropping them heavily toward my sides. "Nobody really understands what I'm going through."

He giggled as if he knew I'd say that and responded with, "I understand what you're going through, baby girl. Just remember that you can't please everybody, so worry about pleasing yourself."

When my mother walked in, I was relieved to get some of the pressure off of me due to sharing my feelings with my father. I only hoped he wouldn't bring it up to her. All that would do is cause them to double team me and drag out the process longer. In my mind, anything I was going to do depended on me and me only. Besides, they didn't care about fitting in anymore because they had each other, and all I had was Marissa.

"Hey!" she said cheerfully before closing and locking the door behind her. "What you two talking about?"

"Nothin!" I said speaking for my father too. He turned around nodded his head slowly, as if to say he knew what I was doing, and I was relieved. My mother thought everything could be solved by coming up to the school. And the last time she did that I was so embarrassed, I played hooky for a week.

"I know what that means," she said smiling at us both. "You guys don't want to tell me. It don't even matter, I love ya'll anyway," she laughed.

Whenever she smiled anybody within eye distance had to smile too. She had one of them Janet Jackson smiles that warmed your heart. She always told me that I had it too but I never believed her. Maybe if I had someone who loved me as much as daddy loved her, I could smile that brightly. My mother was still very beautiful after all these years. Her hazel eyes and dark brown skin didn't have a wrinkle on it, and she looked far younger than the 42 years she actually was. She was 5'7 and her legs were still perfectly fit from all those years that she and Mamma Maria would go to *Latin Night* at The Chateau in D.C., and dance the night away. The only reason they stopped going was because Mamma Maria's so called boyfriend came into the picture, and demanded that she stop.

The best thing about my parents being together was that after all of this time, was how they were still *in* love. You could see it the moment you saw them together. Mamma and daddy couldn't keep their hands off of each other, so witnessing it was border-line mushy and cute. They'd met in school and had been childhood sweethearts ever since.

Mamma put her purse, bags and keys down, walked over to me and daddy and planted warm kisses on both of us. Mine on my cheek and my daddy's on his lips. I secretly prayed that I'd find somebody to love me the way daddy loved her, so that someday I'd have a family of my own.

"I got some new clothes for you, baby!" She said picking the bags up off the floor, and placing them on the glass table in front of where we sat.

"I thought you were gonna take me with you?"

"You were in school, Kiante," she explained. "So I decided to go by myself."

I noticed the bags were from Macy's which happened to be one of my favorite stores but that didn't matter because she always managed to choose the most hideous things in the store. I watched her rummage through the large plastic bags before she grabbed a shirt, knocking the other bags on the floor. I hurriedly picked them up and sat them down on the carpet beside her as I eye-balled the ugly green and red shirt she dangled in her hands. "You like it?"

My eyes roamed to the blue jean skirt I was wearing and then onto my father. If I told her how I really felt he'd be angry with me. I didn't want to hurt her feelings, but I also knew that if she asked me again, I would have to tell her the truth. With the problems I was having now, there was no way I'd make matters worse by wearing that shit to school. It looked like something Freddy Krueger's wife would wear.

"Well?" She said shaking the shirt in front of me. "You like it or what?"

She was excited as if the shirt was for her. My mother stayed buying me things that I didn't like knowing full well I preferred the money instead. I think she tried to dress me because Mamma Maria always knew what to buy for Lucia and Marissa and she tried to compete.

"It's okay, mamma," I responded dryly. "I woulda preferred the money though."

Her face immediately saddened. I hated to see her this way but she needed to know how I really felt.

Daddy seeing my mother's reaction said, "Come here, baby." My mother took his out-stretched hand and sat in the middle of us on the couch. "Kiante will like it when she puts it on. You'll see."

"No I won't, daddy! It's a hot mess!"

"Kiante," he said picking up the baritone in his voice. "You *will* like it once you put it on. Besides, you haven't even seen if she has something for you to wear with it in the bags."

My father's lies made my mother feel better instantly. She leaned into him as he gently kissed her on the cheek. Just like I said, he had a way of making everything better, but this time it was for her, not for me. When he winked at me I knew exactly what his plan was. Later on tonight he'd probably sneak into my room with the receipt in hand so that I could swap all of that crap out for what I really wanted.

"And, Kiante," he said as he one armed hugged my mother. "You got that," he continued referring about the money.

"Thank you, daddy."

When I thought about returning the clothes, and daddy giving me the money, the ultimate plan popped into my mind. If it goes as planned, I'd be able to steer everything in my direction for a change.

NOTHIN LIKE ME

KIANTE

"**Y**ou got to do it like this, Kiante," Marissa said as she bucked her hips on top of the bed as if she was fucking her man. "Then you got to throw your hair back...move your hips in a circular motion, put your hands on your waist, and moan - *Ooooh baby. Ooooo Baby! I'm about to cum. I'm about to cum.*"

"You loud as shit!" I laughed feeling embarrassed by her show.

"You keep worrying about everybody else, and you ain't gonna never find a man. I'm trying to hook you up. Give you my tips on how I make them cum *every time.*"

"I know how to please a man so you ain't got to show me shit!"

"So you know how to please a man huh?" she asked in an unbelieving tone.

"Yes I do!"

"Well show me."

"What?" I asked as I was beginning to eat my own words.

"You said you know how to please a man, she continued as she sat up on the bed and looked at me while I was still lying down. "So I want you to show me."

Reluctantly I sat straight up, got on my knees and for a second stared at Marissa's colorful bedspread. There were greens, reds, and blues throughout it. I was trying to get my game plan down because for real, I knew I couldn't fuck with Marissa when it came to having sex. She was far more experienced than I was.

"Well I don't usually ride them," I started as I lay back down instead. "I usually give it to 'em hardcore on my back."

"Hardcore, huh?"

"Yep!"

"Well show me what you got, mami!" She laughed. "I'm ready and willing to learn."

Lying flat on my back I thought about how it felt the first time me and Jamal had sex. When I remembered how badly it hurt because I was a virgin, I thought about the fourth time instead. The fourth time I was loosened up and was even able to push back into him and move my hips a little.

Pulling my knees to my chest I was getting ready to get into performance when she said, "Move, bitch! You gonna make a nigga go soft with your procrastinating and shit."

"I'm getting ready to, dang!" I yelled at her. "Stop being a freak." She acted like I was fucking her or something. For real, I think Marissa could *easily* go both ways.

I grabbed my ankles and put my sock covered feet flat on the bed. My knees were straight in the air and I started rotating my hips around and around and pumping my waist back and forth. I was surprised at how comfortable it felt and was even getting aroused. That was until I saw Marissa laughing.

"What's funny, bitch?!" I asked her as I lifted my head to look at her face.

"You don't fuck like that," she informed me. "You look like somebody pokin' needles in your back under the bed or somethin'". She took her hands, opened my legs, and almost lost a finger when I snapped them back shut.

"What you doin?!" I yelled at her.

"Don't flatter yourself, sweetie," she giggled. "I'm not trying to fuck you. I wanna do the next man you with a favor. I'm hookin' you up!"

"What you talkin' about, Marissa?"

"For starters, you look like you're having a seizure. Soften your face a little."

"What you mean *soften* my face?"

"Think about how Beyonce looks in her videos. Her face don't look like this," she said as she crossed her eyes and moved her head like a chicken. "It's soft, seductive and sexy."

"Whatever."

"I'm serious, Kiante. And…you have to relax, mami! You're not getting a pap smear you're getting dick! Respect it! Loosen up!"

With that I spread my knees slowly. She was on her knees in between my legs and softly began to maneuver my hips. I prayed nobody would come in and see us like this because there was no explaining it. "Now when you move, pretend you're dancing to your favorite song or something."

"Okay," I said keeping my eyes on her.

"That's it," she continued as I listened to Usher's *You Got It Bad* song on her stereo.

"Is that door locked?" I asked.

"You act like we doin' something! Calm down and pay attention to my voice. Close your eyes," she said not answering my questions and pressing my hips further against the bed. Although she wasn't on top of me, this felt awkward. For a minute.

"Now…," she started. "Rotate your hips and your hips only! Not your back and neck like you did earlier!"

I followed her instructions and listened to Usher sing. This time instead of thinking about Jamal, I thought about her sister's boyfriend Hempay. I imagined he was on top of me and was slowly fucking me as I clawed his back. I could smell the cologne he wore at school and could even feel his cold chain brush against my face. It felt so real that I began to feel all warm and tingly inside. There's something about him that I couldn't resist. I wanted just one moment with him. My body was no longer mine, it was all his.

"Damn, girl!" she yelled waking me out of my thoughts. "You almost tried to get me. Who were you thinkin' about?"

I was embarrassed because for a minute I allowed my mind and body to go someplace else. "None of your business."

"Ummm, Um," she said shaking her head. "You act like you wanted me or something."

"You wish," I said kicking her away from me with my feet as she fell back on the bed. "You the one who wanted to play sex games."

After our little sex scene, we were now lying across the bed on our backs talking about our love lives or lack there of. She had Mary J. Blige's *My Life* CD, pumping in the background to prevent Lucia and her friends from hearing our business in the living room. The moment I started singing along with my favorite part, this crazy girl busts out and says that Dinky came up to the barber shop the other day to approach her sister's ex-boyfriend Damon. Why was she just telling me now? We didn't have any secrets. And what happened to Chris, who she claimed she all of a sudden liked despite me sucking his dick in the Laundromat? This girl had too many men and too many issues.

"Well what did he do?"

"Who?" She asked as she attempted to pull the white Rocawear baby-t over her slightly protruding stomach. Mamma Maria had cooked earlier, and we were both still a little full. "Dinky or Damon?" she continued as her belly won the tug of war and remained uncovered.

"Wait a minute…is Chris totally out of the picture or not? Because as far as I knew you was dealin' with him."

"You didn't know?"

"How would I know Marissa if you don't tell me!"

"Well I'm feeling Damon now."

"You are a mess! So what you gonna do?"

"About which one?"

"All of them! Stop acting like it's not a big deal either! I should kick your ass anyway for not telling me you are fuckin' your sister's ex!"

"You been so caught up in the fact that Jamal dumped you, that I didn't want to say anything."

"First of all Jamal did not dump me, and second of all you're lying. I wasn't trippin' off of him. He do his thing and I do mine."

"Yes you were, Kiante," she responded as she sat up and turned down the music slightly. "Every time I bring something up about Dinky or Chris you'd say, *at least you got two boyfriends cuz I ain't got shit.*"

She was right. Sometimes when she talked about Dinky or Chris, I was reminded that I was lonely and miserable. And now with Jamal blackmailing me by saying he was going to tell people I gave him a disease if I didn't give him money, things were getting even more out of control. I wasn't about to tell Marissa either, because I had a feeling that although she was my best friend, I wasn't hers.

"Well what are you gonna do?" I asked ignoring her last comment.

"Before I tell you anything I wanna know did you tell anybody I was dealing with Damon?"

I was insulted she even thought I'd do something like that to begin with. Not to mention she was the only friend I had and up until this point, I only knew about Chris and Dinky.

"What I look like telling anybody you were messing with Damon when I ain't even know? The last I heard he was *just* shaving your pussy. And who in the fuck would I tell if you did mention it to me?"

"You right," she responded partially believing me. "It just don't make any sense that Dinky knows when he don't even go to school."

"What about Crystal," I asked sitting up in the bed. "Did you tell that loud mouthed bitch about him? You talk to her almost as much as you talk to me."

She was silent for a little while but she still lied to me. I knew right then she told her. "Naw…I ain't say nothing to her about it."

"Yeah okay, Marissa," I said shaking my head. "So who you gonna deal with? And don't tell me both of them because if they find out, you can get really hurt!" I said as I picked her phone book up off the bed, and looked through it. She had every boy's number she ever met in there since we were in elementary school. If she lost it, she'd probably lose her mind right along with it.

"I don't know what I'm gonna do about Dinky, but I know I'm not cuttin' Damon off. Chris' ass *been* out the picture because he got too many other girls he be dealing with at school. He think he a playa and that I don't know 'bout them bitches. I'm playin' his ass the way he think he playin' me."

"We all know he's a dog," I reminded her. "But its obvious Dinky still likes you," I responded as one of the pages of the phone book dropped out and fell onto the bed. As I placed it back in the book I said, "So what you gonna do about him? He deserves to know what's goin' on."

"I ain't want to say nothin'," she started as she stood up and walked toward her mirror. "But I think Dinky's gay."

"What you talkin' about?" I knew exactly what she meant, but I never thought she realized it.

"Like I said, I think he's gay! That day he came up to the shop, he was wearing a pair of jeans tighter than the ones I got on now," she continued slapping her ass. "What straight man you know, wears tight anything?"

"Don't even try it, Marissa! He's been wearing tight ass jeans forever."

"But a pink shirt, too, Kiante?!" She asked as her arms moved in an over dramatic fashion. "You gotta know he's gay."

"Marissa, he's still your man."

"Did you hear me?" she asked. "The boy wears pink shirts? I'm surprised you couldn't tell," she continued. "He's more worried about fashion and clothes than we are. Plus he eats pussy too good to be straight."

"What him eatin' pussy real good got to do with him being gay? Usually gay men don't want to see no parts of a pussy let alone eat one."

"It got a lot to do with it if you *prefer* to eat pussy *instead* of fuckin'."

"I don't care what you say," I continued holding my ground. "Dinky took care of you."

"You mean us," she laughed pointing and me and then her. "That's why you like him."

"That's one of the reasons," I admitted. "But he really loves you. If you leave him, maybe he will turn gay."

"I'm not no Straight Man Maker!"

"I still like Dinky for you. Anyway, what's gonna happen when Lucia finds out you're dealing with Damon? You know she gonna kick your ass!"

"She already found out."

"You lyin!" Once again this bitch held out on some serious information. "What happened?"

"Well you know I played hooky the other day right?"

I nodded my head yes and hit her in the leg when she sat beside me. I remember that day specifically because she had me outside for 30 minutes after school waiting to take her home. Eventually I said fuck it and rolled out. Today was the first time I'm hearing the reason she left me hanging.

"Well he came home with me. We had just finished having sex and everything when this bitch pops up because she was ditching school too."

"Hempay was with her?" I asked still a little jealous of their relationship.

"You know it!"

"I know she went off on your ass when she saw Damon! You know how serious she was about him."

"Well, luckily for her she knew better than to fuck wit' me."

"Marissa, please," I laughed. "You have always been afraid of Lucia."

"Don't be fooled, sweetie," she responded. "Lucia know what time it is."

"Whatever," I responded waving her off.

"Anyway, Damon was just getting ready to leave but as he opened my bedroom door, Lucia and Hempay walked in the front," she started whispering heavily but in a low voice. "She looked like she wanted to cry when she saw us together."

"I knew she still had feelings for him! She stay going down the barbershop to get her eyes arched but all the while claiming *he* wanted her back. That girl has a full hot wax kit right in her room! She can do her own eyebrows."

"I know, right?" Marissa laughed. "But instead of her leaving us alone, what does she do? She starts telling him that it was fucked up that he was messing with a *little* girl. I reminded her ass right there she wasn't but two years older than me. You know what made me really mad?"

"What?"

"My sister wasn't mad about him messing with her sister, but the fact that he fucked a little girl." She paused. "Fuck her ass!"

"I'm surprised she ain't hit him!"

"How would that look like with Hempay right there? I mean, what was she going to do, be mad I was fucking her ex-boyfriend with her current boyfriend standing right there?"

"What did Hempay do?" I asked.

"He said, *main man, you gotta leave.* But he was already on his way out the door. You know Hempay never liked Damon because if Lucia didn't break up with him, she would've never given Hempay the time of day."

"Damn!"

"But it ain't like Hempay's pockets are not longer than Damon's! Don't get me wrong, Damon do alright at the shop, but he can't compete with no hustler. You should see all that shit in Lucia's closet."

"I ain't got to see that," I said wishing I was in her place. "Look at her car. She got everything! A body, face, clothes and the man!"

"Get off her shit," Marissa said pushing me on the arm. She and Lucia were so physical. Nothing could be said with *just* words. It was always words followed by or before some kind of physical contact like a push or shove.

"I'm not on her shit."

"Yes you are," she said. "I think you want to be my sister."

"Doubt it!"

"Yeah okay!" She said getting up again to change C.D.'s. "But I fucked Damon's brains out."

"You's a nasty bitch!" I laughed.

"Call it what you want but I'm feelin' Damon now. His dick stays hard and he always on point. Lucia got a fine ass nigga so I don't even know why she trippin'."

"Right!" I responded a little too excitingly about Lucia having a fine ass nigga. "Hempay has to be good in bed," I blurted out. "He is entirely too fine."

Before she could respond, Lucia walked into the room without knocking. "What ya'll doin in here?" She asked, wearing a pair of black Gucci shorts, black Puma tennis and a white BeBe t-shirt. I pouted when I was reminded again that she could wear a curtain and still look sexy in it.

"We're mindin', Lucia!" Marissa yelled throwing a pair of balled up socks at her. She ducked just before they hit her face.

"If that would've hit me, your fat ass would've been laying on the floor right now."

"Get out of my room, Lucia!"

"Don't even try it, girl, cuz you stay coming into my room!"

"Yeah right! For five seconds before you're throwing me back out again."

"Don't flatter yourself because I'm only in here to borrow that new Baby Phat outfit you picked up last month. Me, Raven, Karen and Hempay are getting ready to go to the movies tonight."

"Lucia, you got all that shit in your room. Why you wanna wear my shit?"

"Because I do!"

"Well too bad, so sad," Marissa responded sarcastically.

"I need to wear that tonight!"

"I'm sorry," she stopped looking her up and down. "But what does that have to do with me again?" She continued placing her hands on her hips.

"Stop playing, girl! It ain't like you can fit it. You can barely wear them jeans you got on now. Let me do you a favor and show you how it should look when you finally are able to squeeze into it."

"For your information I *can* fit it," she lied. I knew she was lying because just the other day she tried to put it on and mentioned she had to drop a few pounds to be able to do it. So unless she was on some amazing ass diet, she was bound to have the same problem today.

But instead of Lucia leaving, she called her bluff, "Well if you can fit it, prove it!" she responded reaching into her closet and throwing the one piece skirt outfit onto the bed.

"I ain't got to prove nothin' to you, bitch!"

"You ain't got to prove nothin' because you're lying!"

"Stop picking, Lucia! If she don't want to wear it she ain't got to." I said intruding into their conversation. "You're just showing off so your friends can hear you in the living room."

"Showing off?" She sang drawing each word out. "What I got to show off for? I'm not you!" She continued spinning around so that I could get another look at the body I already knew she had. "I don't have to show off shit because I'm not the one lying about being able to squeeze my fat ass into an outfit I can't even wear. And I'm not the one who's so pressed to be with somebody else's ex-boyfriend either."

"Let me find out you still mad because your ex-boyfriend, Damon chose me!" Marissa responded shooting knives into her sister's heart.

"I'm not even trippin' over his weak ass. Don't forget, I dumped him."

"That's not what I heard," Marissa winked. "I heard you were so mad about losing him, you ran into the arms of Hempay."

"You wish I would have to run into the arms of anybody! All I know is this, you can't get into that outfit."

I had all intentions of going at Lucia some more to save Marissa from further embarrassment but when I looked out the corner of my eyes, I saw her getting undressed and preparing to take her sister up on the challenge. I shook my head slowly as I noticed she was already having problems getting out of the size 8 jeans she was wearing for her size 10 frame. Now Marissa wasn't a big girl at all, but I knew for a fact that she wasn't getting up in that size 4 spread out across the bed. The only reason she bought it was because it was the only size left. Knowing it wouldn't work Marissa still attempted to prove her wrong. She squeezed everything into the outfit as the seams fought to stay together.

When Marissa made it happen Lucia said, "Button it up!" She was trying to conceal her laughter but she couldn't. She loved how as usual, she could manipulate her into doing things she wanted her to do. I think that although Marissa claimed her sister got on her nerves, she wanted to be like her so much, that she'd even go as far as to be with somebody she use to date. "It ain't fully on until you button it all the way up!" Lucia continued.

"You said get into it!" Marissa responded trying hard not to breathe. "You didn't say nothin' about buttoning it up."

"Be for real, Marissa!" Lucia responded projecting her voice. "You know what I meant. If you can't do it say you can't do it. It's obvious you're having a hard time anyway!"

Instead of leaving it alone, Lucia buttoned the outfit slowly, holding in her breath as if she was lifting weights. When each one was closed, pieces of her skin poked out between wholes over and under the buttons.

"S...see?" she said holding her arms out on her sides. The moment she raised them, the outfit made a ripping sound as it came apart right before our eyes. Suddenly it was me who was trying to conceal my laughter while Lucia proceeded to laugh out loud in her face.

"Oh shit...Raven and Karen!" Lucia laughed hysterically while opening the bedroom door. "Ya'll got to come see this shit!"

It sounded like a stampede as they both came running into the room. Raven and Karen always made me feel uncomfortable and Marissa felt the same. They were the epitome of everything I wanted to be at school. The moment I was around them, I immediately became nervous and intimidated hoping they wouldn't say anything that would make me feel worse than I already did about myself. Whenever I'd try to speak to them at school, they'd shoot me a look to remind me that I wasn't worthy of their friendship.

"Check this out ya'll," Lucia started. "I asked her what's up with the outfit she had in the closet right..." she paused.

"No, you asked me can you wear it, bitch!" Marissa corrected her. "Get it right!" She continued as she took the tattered and torn outfit off revealing her half naked body.

"Whatever," she paused feeling slightly embarrassed that she asked her sister to borrow anything. "I asked her to put the outfit on right, and she squeezes her fat ass into it and rips it to pieces."

"Marissa when you gonna lose some weight?" Raven asked as if she was concerned. "This has gone on far too long."

"Yeah...you need to stop looking at the track at school and start running on it."   "I hate you, Lucia! I hope you die!" Marissa yelped.

"Fuck you!" she shot back.

"One day you gonna get what the fuck you deserve, too!"

"You don't mean that," I added as Raven and Karen glanced at me. Before I said anything, I don't even think they knew I was in the room.

"Yes I do, too! She think she betta than everybody else when for real, she's not! And before she dies the bitch is gonna get what she deserves. Sister or not!"

"Betta than everybody else?" Lucia repeated.

"Yeah. And what does she think is betta," Raven added as she picked up what was left of the dress. "Because before you can even be in the competition, you have to be in your league."

"I didn't ask you anyway!" Marissa screamed. It was as if she had gotten something off of her chest. She was so loud, that it startled all of them, even herself.

"I'm only telling the truth," Raven snickered due to her behavior. "And the truth is, you are getting a little on the chunky side!" Raven continued as she walked up to her and squeezed a piece of Marissa's flesh around her waist.

Raven was short but the loudest girl I ever met in my entire life. She had really light skin and freckles all over her face. Although her waist was tiny, her ass was huge, and she thought that gave her the right to tell somebody else what they didn't have or what they needed to do with their bodies.

"Fuck you, Raven cuz you ain't so thin either," Marissa announced as she looked at me to help her out. But I couldn't say anything, I was already sweating hoping they wouldn't direct their insults toward me.

"That may be true, but at least I buy the clothes that *fit*, not the ones I *want*!" She said smacking her tongue.

"Yeah, Marissa," Karen added as she sat on the bed causing me to lose balance since I was sitting on the edge. "What possessed you to pick a size too small for you?"

By this time Lucia had already left the room, still Raven and Karen remained behind.

Karen was 5'7 and very pretty so when she got out on you, you felt bad about it. She had mahogany colored skin and hair the same texture as Lucia and Marissa's. She ran track so her legs were fit and she had a stomach so flat and tight, you could bounce a quarter on it.

"I want both of ya'll fake ass bitches out of my room! Lucia is out there," she continued as she jumped up from her bed and grabbed Karen off the bed by her arms to lead her out.

"I know you must've lost your mind by putting your hands on me!" Karen said as she stepped up to Marissa. On instinct I stood right beside her and I don't even know why. As rude as they were, I knew that if you got them wrong, you would never be a part of their crew, and I wanted that more than anything. "And what the fuck you gonna do?" She asked me.

"Come on ya'll," I paused looking at everyone. "This is getting out of hand."

"Getting out of hand?" Raven asked stepping up to me. "Don't you mean getting out of mouth."

"What?"

"Come on now...," she continued giving Karen high fives. "We all know how you get down, *Kiante*. Word around school is that when you're in the Laundromat, you're washing more than just clothes.

"I don't know what you talkin' about."

"Sure you do, sweetie," Raven added. "You know exactly what I'm talking about."

"You're a whore and your little friend right here's a backstabber." Karen giggled. "No wonder you're friends."

"I'm not trippin' off of shit ya'll say," Marissa said walking away from them.

I couldn't move, and because I couldn't, they kept coming at me. I didn't even realize I was crying until they started pointing at me.

"And she's a cry baby!" Raven laughed.

"What are ya'll doin' to this girl?!" Hempay asked coming into the room, his eyes fixed on me and the state I was in.

As sad as I was, I couldn't get over how handsome he was *every* time I saw him. I was tempted to cry harder in the hopes he would touch me or maybe even hug me. I thought better of it because I didn't want to appear weaker than I already was. Hempay's hair was freshly braided and his new jeans hung on his body perfectly. The red Sean Jean jacket he had on with the white-t made him look edible.

"Ain't nobody doin' nothin' to this girl!" Karen said in a flirtingly seductive tone. "You betta mind your business before I fight you." She continued playfully hitting him.

"I'm serious," he said as he grabbed her hand. "Why ya'll in here when we goin' to the movies in a minute?"

"We were just talkin' to them," Raven advised approaching him. "We comin' now."

"Well wait out in the living room."

"Calm down, Hempay," Karen said. "It's not that serious."

"So why you still in here?" He asked daring them with his eyes to say another word.

"We'll see you two around. Come on, Raven." She continued looking at me and Marissa before walking out.

When they both left the room Hempay spoke in a low voice so only I could hear him. "You know they gonna keep fuckin' wit' you if you let 'em, right?"

"Everything was okay. They were just in our business," I said feeling ashamed he thought I couldn't defend myself.

"I'm serious. Don't let them skeezas talk to you any kind of way. Start standin' up for yourself, shawty."

"Alright," I said softly.

"I'm serious," he said sternly. "I'll get up wit' ya'll lada."

REVERSED

When he left I thought about what he said and what I did to warrant being talked down to by them. I came to the realization that they were right. I did play myself by doing what I did to Jamal and them in the laundry room. But I also knew if I played my cards right, things would be changing for me real soon. At least I hoped.

NEW YORK, NEW YORK
KIANTE

I knocked on the Marissa's door three times before J.D. said, "Who is it?!"

"It's Kiante," I said loud enough for him to hear me. "I'm here to see if Marissa is ready for school."

He flung the door open and yelled, "W…W..wait in h…here!" J.D pointed in the living room. He was holding himself up with one wooden crutch. I walked in and closed the door behind me. When I did, I noticed J.D., looked bad. Spit from his broken jaw had fallen onto his light blue shirt and created stains. I was preparing to walk to Marissa's room when he stopped me in my tracks.

"You d..d..don't la…live here so st…stop acting like it by roaming through m…my house," he said as he held his hand out in front of him.

"Alright J.D.," I told him sitting on the couch. "Can you tell her I'm here then?" I responded with an attitude.

"Wa…One d..day you gonna get wa… what's coming to you. You and Hem….pp..pay."

"Are you threatening me?"

He didn't respond. Instead he screamed, "Marisssssa." Spit fell from his mouth again. Apparently the "S" sound was hard for him. I felt a nauseous feeling take over me as I watched him in disgust. "This bitch is out here!" Afterwards, he walked out the door.

J.D.'s leg never set right after Hempay broke it and neither did his mouth. We barely understood what he was saying half of the time he spoke. It was gross watching him speak because he didn't have full control over his lower jaw so whenever he opened his mouth, slobber would fall out and onto his shirt. He carried a towel around that was really a bib, tucked under his shirt. If you were one of the people he had to hug and it was later in the day, you'd get a whiff of the tart, stale, dried smell of saliva.

I didn't really expect Hempay to do everything he did to him when I told him what J.D did to Mamma Maria a few days back. To be honest, I don't know what I thought he'd do but I hated seeing Mamma Maria being held over the kitchen sink screaming her lungs out while begging him not to slice her throat. Since I was the one who told Hempay and the only one in the kitchen that day to witness J.D.'s rage, Hempay warned him that if he fucked with me, he'd break his other leg.

"Marissa, come on! We gonna be late!" I yelled while sitting in the living room watching TV.

With J.D gone, I could loosen up while waiting on Marissa. Mamma Maria had gone over to my mother's to help her with the garden this morning and Lucia caught a ride with Hempay to school.

"Marissa!" I screamed again. "Hurry the fuck up! What you doin' in there anyway?!"

"I'm coming, girl. Wait a minute!"

"You about to get left!" I threatened for the hundredth time since I'd known her. "You better not be writing in that diary."

She had a thing for recording everything in her pink diary *early* in the morning. Now that would be okay if it was on her personal time, but right now she had me out here waiting! No secret was off limit from that diary, including mine. I often asked her where she kept it for fear of it getting in the wrong hands but she never really told me.

We had 30 minutes to make it to school and it took us 25 minutes to get there without traffic so Marissa was pushing it. She wasn't black so it's not like it took her all day to do her hair like it did me. Fifteen minutes later Marissa appeared wearing these bad ass pair of Rock and Republic jeans with a cute pink Juicy Couture top. She completed her look with a pair of pink Prada boots.

"I see Damon's been lacin' you up," I acknowledged looking her up and down.

"How you know it's Damon?"

I laughed and pushed her away. "Well I know it's not Chris' stingy, broke, tired ass!"

"Don't hold back, Kiante," she said grabbing Lucia's pink Louis Vuitton purse. "Say what you really feel about him," she laughed. "Now I know I look cute today," she responded examining what I was wearing. "But what do you have on?"

I laughed inside because she had no idea of what I had in store. I called it the "Ultimate Plan". Today was the first day my little idea would be placed into action. The only messed up part was that I wasn't able to include Marissa in on what I was doing. In all honesty the full plan recently popped in my head. With this new idea, nobody could doubt that I was a *new* person. As far as Marissa was concerned, if she couldn't keep her own secrets safe, I knew there was no way in the world she'd be able to keep mine. So if everything was going to work in my favor, I had to keep my business to myself.

"I didn't feel like getting dressed today."

"You could've worn anything better than that, Kiante. I mean come on. You're wearing a pair of raggedy sweat pants and an oversized shirt."

"Like I said, I didn't feel like getting dressed. Besides, I was up all night talkin' to my boyfriend on the phone." I left her with that as I walked toward the door.

"Wait a minute, bitch!" she yelled coming behind full speed. "You ain't tell me you had a *new* man!"

"You didn't ask."

"Well, who you fuckin' wit' now?! It's not Angry Andre is it? Cuz I know he likes you." She closed the front door and we were preparing to walk down the stairwell.

"No it's not. You don't know him," I said as if I was uninterested in talking about anything. "And aren't you forgetting something?"

"What?"

"To lock the door."

She ran back upstairs to lock the door and ran back down the steps behind me. It took everything in my power not to laugh at the way she was acting. Marissa couldn't take me holding back a secret when just the other day, she gave me the 411 days after the fact. We jumped in my car.

"Kiante, that's fucked up!" After clicking her seat belt, she gave me the *look*. I could tell she was growing more and more annoyed at my hiding of information. It didn't help that I gave her no indication that I intended on telling her his name. "Kiante!"

"Yes, precious?" I smiled.

"Are you gonna tell me what's up or not? I can start holding back stuff, too."

"You been doin' it, Marissa. Anyway, I'm not hiding anything. I'm just not telling you about it."

"Can you at least tell me when this all happened?"

I shook my head no.

"Why you holdin' back?"

Marissa was pestering me but for real, I liked it. "I'm not holding anything back," I said real calmly.

"Is it because I fuck wit' Chris on the side sometimes?"

"Marissa, I could care less about you fuckin' with him on the side, front or back. That nigga's simple! And judging by our convo the other day, you fucks wit' plenty of niggas on the side so why should I be concerned about just one?" I was salty that she tried to carry me as if I was even thinking about him. I was getting over what I did in the Laundromat and most shit rolled off of my chest. The only thing I didn't care for was how she hung out with Chris, Jamal and his new girlfriend at school in my face sometimes.

"Well if you're not trippin' then what's with the silent treatment?"

"Damn, Marissa! I just haven't had the time to tell you that's all and when I get ready to I will! So stop asking me."

"He must be weak anyway because if he was like that, you'd be pressed to let me know his name."

"Is that what you think?" I laughed.

"Yep."

"Marissa, *please*," I started as if she was a little girl who didn't have the slightest idea about life. "Ya'll be fuckin wit' them elementary school niggas, but I have moved on to big timers."

When we pulled into the student parking lot, her eyes were glued onto me. I could tell she wanted to slap me but thought better of it. When we reached the building, Crystal's fake ass came running up to us in the hallway. She was a tall skinny light-skin girl with short curly hair. Puberty was not kind to her. Everything about her was flat but her mouth. I had plans to accidentally bump into her later but this was much better. In order to set things into motion, I needed her mouth to be in full mode.

"Hey, girl!" she said coming up to me. "You playin' hooky today?" Crystal was the kinda person who loved talkin' about people to their face and expected you not to notice or care.

"Hooky? What you talkin' about, Crystal?"

"Your clothes lookin' like you 'bout to go back home or somethin'," she said as if she was a concerned friend instead of a sneaky ass bitch. She was the only person me and Marissa placed on the *Two Word* rule. The Two Word rule usually meant we didn't say more than two words to a person we considered fake, that way they couldn't turn something we said around. But lately even Marissa had been playing her close. Today I would break my own rule because I needed her to run her mouth.

"Crystal, I'm not going home early," I assured her as I continued to walk toward my locker, with her and Marissa following. "I was up all night on the phone talkin' to my new boyfriend and didn't have a chance to get all glamorous for ya'll. But I hope you can, understand." I smiled.

"You've never been glamorous," Crystal laughed. "But I will say you usually dress better than you are today." *I swear I can't stand this bitch.*

"As long as my man is not complaining, I'm not either."

"Your man?" She asked looking at Marissa for confirmation. I could tell right then that they talked more than Marissa let off. "When you get a man?"

Talk about somebody's antennas popping up. She couldn't wait to find out who I was talking about so she could put it in the verbal gossip paper at school. This bitch could spread the word faster than an email.

"What's his name?" She inquired as she moved closer to me. Marissa although she was still mad, was listening hard too. Good thing for me I had already thought about this part of my plan. Therefore the answer rolled off my tongue just as smoothly as her question.

When I thought about his name, I knew it had to be one that screamed New York, hustler, re-spect and money. With that I said, "Blaze. He's from New York."

Slamming my locker shut both of their mouths dropped open. New York niggas were hard to come by especially if you were in high school.

So the fact that I had one made them jealous of me and had them doubting I was telling the truth.

"He hustle or something?" Crystal inquired in an envious tone.

"What you think?" I giggled as I looked at her sideways. "I swear ya'll act so young. Just cuz you in high school don't mean you have to act that way."

"Well, if he pumpin' like that, how come I can't tell?" She asked as she observed my clothes. Little did she know a wardrobe change was part of my plan, too. But it was cute how she tried to play me once again. You had to be tough to deal with Crystal. The average person would've cried or knocked all her teeth out but I was tired of playing the victim.

"When he moves down here you *will* be able to tell then because we're getting married. Anyway we're putting up money for a new place so there will be plenty of time to dress fly."

"Kiante, you need to stop lyin!" Crystal spat stomping her feet. "You know damn well your parents not gonna let you get married so young. And to a hustler at that? Get out of here with that bullshit!"

"I ain't say we were getting married tomorrow. But trust and believe, it will be over the next two years," I said as I giggled a little in her face. "And Crystal stop thinkin' you know every thing that goes on in my house. Unlike some people," I said looking at Marissa. "I don't tell you everything that goes on with me. And I don't have to say anything else. You'll be able to see when he comes to town how I roll. Now if you will excuse me, I'm runnin' late for class."

Their mouths dropped open again as I walked off and left them both hanging. Later on that day it was broadcast across the entire school that I was *supposedly* fucking with this New York nigga. One girl, who didn't know it was me, was telling me about the rumor. I had to inform her that the rumor was true and the girl she was talking about was right in front of her. Right now nothing I said held weight because my clothes were raggedy and I was known as a bamma. But in a minute, all of that would be changing.

THINGS WERE CHANGING
KIANTE

A week after I told Crystal I was dating somebody from Brooklyn New York, I had quickly became the buzz around school. Most people thought I was lying and a few of them wanted to see Blaze in person before they made up their minds. The toughest part was having to distance myself from Marissa, because I had to appear busy with Blaze at all times. Whenever she called I told her to call back, and that I was on the other line with him. It was tough at first because we are so close.

Although I wasn't there for her lately, I felt that if she was truly my friend, she'd understand I had a life too. The same way I understood when she wanted to see Chris, despite what he did to me. Marissa wasn't the only person trippin' about my so-called boyfriend because suddenly, Jamal was showing me extra attention too. And when I blew him off, he threatened to blackmail me with the STD thing again. I already paid him the money he asked for and everything. Yet he still had the nerve to ask me if we could kick it again like we use to. When I reminded him about his new girlfriend, he said that what she didn't know wouldn't hurt her. I just walked away and left him standing. He was no longer a part of my plans and I wanted to keep it that way.

Even though I'd been brushing my best friend off, today Marissa stopped being mad at me, and asked me to take her to the Laundromat in Maryland. Although she had one downstairs, I knew she called because she missed me and I decided to take her up on her offer.

I hadn't been over their house in over a week, and it almost felt like I'd been away from home, my second home. The moment I pulled up and saw Hempay's truck parked in the alley next to Lucia's car my heart fluttered. There was no denying that I wanted him. I kept my feelings private because I realized I never had a chance with him to begin with. I also noticed that lately he had been giving me the cold treatment at school for whatever reason. I figured something was on his mind because when I asked him if everything was okay, he'd say it was kosher. I kinda missed him calling me pretty, making me laugh and most of all, coming to my rescue when I needed him.

"Come in, Brooklyn," Lucia said in a sassy tone as she opened the door for me. She was jealous already about the rumor I started about Blaze. It was funny to me because I hadn't even given her a reason to be hatin' yet.

"Hey, Lucia," I said closing the door behind myself.

"I'll let Marissa know you're here."

"Where she at? In the room?" I asked as I walked toward Marissa's bedroom. "I can go get her."

"No, you can't," she responded stopping me dead in my tracks. "*I'll* go get her. You just wait right here."

I couldn't get over how lately I'd become less welcome around here. In the past I had full reign over this house including access to the fridge. Now they were treating me like I was a complete stranger.

"Okay," I said giving off a fake smile. When I saw Hempay sitting in the living room watching T.V.

I walked over to him, tapped him on the leg and took my place in the chair directly across from where he sat.

"What you watchin'?"

Silence.

I frowned. Not only did he ignore me, but he didn't even look in my direction. Briefly I thought about everything I did and said at school and I couldn't come up with one single reason for why he would treat me the way that he had been. Instead of guessing, I decided to confront him about it before

Lucia and Marissa came into the living room and we were no longer alone.

"Did I do somethin' to you, Hempay?" I whispered as I leaned in toward him so that he could hear me.

"No." His answer was short and to the point. I can't lie; I felt some kind of way about that.

"No?" I asked hoping he'd elaborate.

"I said no," he responded before cutting his eyes at me, and looking back at the TV.

I glanced at the television briefly to see what he was looking at. When I saw it was the news, I knew he wasn't into it as much as he appeared to be.

"Then why aren't you talkin' to me no more?"

"Look I said, we cool."

"If we cool I can't tell, Hempay," I laughed happy he said a sentence that consisted of something else besides *no*. "I thought you were my big brother."

"From what I understand, you don't need me to look after you no more."

"What is that supposed to mean?" I pleaded.

Just then Mamma Maria came out of her bedroom and walked into the living room.

"Hey, *mija!*" Her voice was cheerful and it felt out of place considering the mood in the living room between me and Hempay was heavy. "Where you been?"

"I've been at home." For the first time ever, Mamma Maria was irritating the hell out of me.

Don't get me wrong. I love her, but I had some questions that needed to be answered.

"The girls tell me you have a new man now," she continued in an upbeat tone. "Is it true?"

"Yes," I said as Hempay glanced in my direction. For some reason answering yes felt uncomfortable with him sitting there.

"That's great! *Well*, let me finish cooking," she responded wiping her hands on the towel she carried on her shoulder. "You coming over later for dinner?"

"I'll try, Mamma Maria," I said hoping she'd get lost so that we could finish our conversation.

"Okay, *mija*." She said kissing me on my cheek before disappearing into the kitchen. When the yellow, green and red housecoat she wore was out of sight, I directed my attention back at Hempay.

Twisting my body back in his direction I said, "Can we be cool like we use to be?"

"I said we was 'aight, Kiante," he said shaking his head. "So what you trippin' off of?"

My nose was stinging again and I could tell I was on the verge of crying. I hated that I was so emotional *all* the time. Why do I have to care so much about every single thing people said to me?

Everybody else can go their entire lives not giving a fuck, but not me.

"Hempay, can you at least tell me why you're acting this way? If it's something I did…the least you could do is tell me."

"You didn't do anything!"

"Well then talk to me!" I know I was begging but I couldn't help myself, a part of me felt as if I was losing a best friend for no reason. After he didn't respond I continued. "Hempay…can I at least have a chance to tell you my side of the story? Because it's obvious somebody has lied to you about something."

"Since you keep askin' questions I'll tell you," he said looking at me and then back at the TV. I could tell he was having a hard time looking at me but I didn't know why. "What's this I hear about you fuckin' wit' some NY cat?"

"Huh?" I heard his question but it caught me off guard. I decided to answer it so that we could get to what my relationship had to do with him.

"I'm just sayin'," he said sounding as if he was trying to think of a reason for being mad. "You too young to be fuckin' wit' some old ass nigga. I heard he was thirty or somethin' years old."

"He is."

"Well I thought you were betta than that."

"Better than what?"

"Don't you know New York niggas ain't gonna do nothin' but play you?"

"He's good to me, Hempay."

"I don't want to hear that shit! Cuz if he was good to you, he'd be here wit' you. He probably got mad bitches in NY and every city in between."

"He's…"

"And then you marrying this clown, too?!" He asked cutting me off.

I wasn't sure, but I had a feeling he was jealous of my relationship. Because every time he'd say something about him, he'd get madder and madder. If he got any louder, Lucia, Mamma Maria and Marissa would probably hear him.

"He's not like that," I responded. Truthfully I didn't feel right arguing over somebody who wasn't even real. "Like I said, Blaze really cares about me."

"You actin' just like a whore. I had you pegged different than that."

That hurt. It was similar to the feeling I had when my father told me he was disappointed in me for fighting at school but worse.

"I'm not a whore, Hempay. He loves me and I love him."

"How you know about love? You ain't nothing but a kid." He shot back.

"So are you." My answer was soft and still careful. I was trying to get him not to be mad at me, not make him angrier. "I mean…we're the same age."

"Listen," he said as he stood up and walked toward the door. "As long as you fuckin' wit' dude, somebody I'm sure will hurt you, I ain't got shit to say to you no more."

"But why?" I asked standing up and gently grabbing his arm. "Just tell me what you're feeling." I wasn't sure but something told me Hempay cared about me. Little old knocked kneed me.

"Is everything okay?" Mamma Maria asked as she wiped her hands on the towel she threw over her left shoulder. She looked at the hand I had on Hempay and then at both of us. It was clear she heard the commotion but not what was said. "Are you two okay?"

"Yeah, everything's cool, Ma," he responded looking dead in my eyes. "I was just leaving." And then he shook me off of him and left, causing my hand to drop down by my side. I watched him dodge out of the door before Lucia appeared in the living room.

"Where Hempay say he was goin'?" She questioned. "Did he say he was coming back?"

"I don't know where he's going, Lucia," I told her shrugging my shoulders. With that she ran down the hallway calling his name.

I sat down on the sofa thinking about everything that just went down. Hempay was giving me the third degree about my make-believe boyfriend like I was *his* girl. Part of me loved the attention and the other part of me didn't like the idea of us no longer being close. Outside of when J.D. put his hands on Mamma Maria, I'd never seen Hempay in such a fucked up mood. I hated thinking that part of his mood change was because of me.

Five minutes later Marissa came in the living room. She had a thing for having me wait for her while she was on the phone. But today her rudeness paid off because I had a chance to talk to Hempay alone.

When we drove to the Laundromat all I thought about was Hempay and why he was so concerned with who I was fuckin' with. No matter how hard I tried, I couldn't come up with a solid explanation why. And then I thought about it, he ain't my man!

Why the fuck should I be trippin? It's time to live my life for me, and anybody who doesn't like it can get out my way or get run over. It was as simple as that.

BIG DAY
KIANTE

Today was the day my plan was goin' into motion! I had Tupac's music on blast in my room while I was getting dressed. I'm sure it was loud enough to wake my parents, but he got me pumped up just by hearing his voice and I needed his energy. I was gonna put everybody who doubted me to shame. I had things arranged so well, that for a minute I forgot Blaze wasn't real.

Saturday I went to the beauty shop without Marissa and got a fly ass haircut. Instead of the dirty brown color I'd worn for years, I was now sportin' an icy coal black hairstyle. I even went to Magic Cindy, even though she was expensive instead of my original stylist to get my perm in. Cindy's fat ass made the nappiest of hair look Indian after she got through with it. Needless to say going to another hairdresser in the same place as your usual one was trouble, and bad politics. But for some reason, that day I didn't care. After I walked out of the doors, I looked exactly how I wanted, like a hustler's wife. The air whipped through my scalp reminding me that my perm was laid. I let it grow out in the front a little, so my Chinese bang could fall over my right eye and the back was short cut and spiky. I was killin' em!

After I put on my clothes I spun around in the mirror. Even if nobody else told me today, I knew I looked hot! It felt similar to the way it does when you have a bangin' ass outfit for the first day of school but better. Today I would finally be able to show them all of the clothes my make-believe man bought for me. I had everybody thinkin' Blaze was comin' into town from New York and it killed them not knowing who he was. To make my plan work, over the past month, since I made the announcement with loud-mouthed ass Crystal, I'd been on a mission to get my gear in order.

How did I pull off my outfit heist? I went to NY for real! NY is the only place you can buy knock off's so tight, they look real. It wasn't hard to find the places to go because Jamaican Lou, a street vendor off of Minnesota Avenue in D.C. told me where to go, just as long as I picked him up a few things. After I begged my daddy to give me $600 over the course of the month, saying that my car had been acting up and needed repairs, I was able to cop everything I needed. He ain't have no problem forking over the money because he'd rather catch the bus than to see me stranded on the street somewhere. Now I had enough clothes to rock strong for three weeks. And, I'd chosen enough pieces so that I could mix and match them and expand it a week longer.

Looking into the mirror one last time, I admired the *new* me. Why didn't I think of this before? My MAC make-up was flawless and there was no way they wouldn't believe me now. I even found a hell of a fake ass engagement ring that on the surface would fool the average high school chick and on glance could fool even Lil Kim. For my outfit of the day, I chose my black one piece knock off Nina Ricci dress with my spiky stiletto Fendi heels. I chose all black because I wanted the ring I had on my finger to be the first thing they saw when I walked through the doors.

I tiptoed into the living room and saw my daddy was up already working on his accounts. He'd managed to save over three thousand dollars. I felt kind of bad when I saw a bank withdrawal receipt from the money I asked him for on the table, came from the savings account. But I needed the money and I knew he'd want me to have it, if he knew what I went through at school. Besides, one of the reasons he was saving the money was to propose to my mother all over again. The way I looked at it, they wouldn't be getting married for another two years anyway...and what I was dealing with was happening right now.

"Whoa," daddy said after seeing me on my way to school. He stood up and greeted me. "My baby looks like a million bucks."

"Finally, daddy," I smiled. "Finally."

"Always, Kiante. You always look beautiful. I'm just happy that you finally realize it."

"Thanks, daddy," I said as I stood on my tiptoes and kissed him on the cheek. Even though I had on heels, I still had to reach up to kiss him. "Love you. Kiss mamma for me when she wakes up."

"I will baby."

I ran out the door and jumped in my car. The rearview mirror was pointed toward my face and I still couldn't get over how pretty I looked. My heart beat wildly as I anticipated the looks on everyone's face. Why is it when you're waiting to show off, you can never get there fast enough? Here I was, dressed like a million bucks, and stuck in the middle of traffic.

It felt weird not having Marissa with me on the way to school. I hadn't seen her all weekend and told her she'd have to get a ride with Lucia today, because I was going to school straight from Blaze's hotel and it would be hard to scoop her up. Of course she begged me for an hour saying Lucia would never take her to school. I knew the real reason she wanted me to pick her up was so she could see him. But I wanted her to be as shocked as everybody else was, when I walked through the school today.

The moment I pulled up, all eyes were on me. It was almost as if I was pushing a Bentley. I looked so good I made my car look better. The moment my high heels hit the concrete in the student parking lot, people were talkin'. Cell phones were poppin' and the word was going on around the school how I looked. It felt amazing. I wasn't walking with my head down, today I had it up.

I got out of the car and walked smoothly to the school doors. "Hey, Kiante!" Some girl yelled who never said two words to me before.

"Hey!" I responded waving my hand in the air.

"Your hair looks pretty, Kiante!" Another girl yelled.

"Thank you!" I replied swinging open the school doors switching from left to right.

The moment I walked to the locker I twirled my Louis Vuitton bag and turned the combination on my lock. I could hear everybody whispering behind me trying to figure out who the *new* girl was at school. I turned around every so often so they could get a look at my face. I had 'em on stuck.

When Hempay walked over to me, my heart dropped. I couldn't look at him and suddenly I felt ashamed at the status I was building on lies and deceit.

"Just so you know," he said pressing his body slightly up against mine as I faced my locker. "I always thought you looked good." After that, he walked off. It was the first thing he said to me in two weeks and for a minute I held on to all of his words.

What did he mean by what he said? Did he think I didn't look good now? Shit! Why does he have to play mind games?! I could still smell the scent of his cologne when Lucia approached me. And apparently she could still smell him, too.

"Was Hempay just here?" She asked looking me up and down.

"I don't know, Lucia," I responded as I turned around to face her. "That's your man not mine."

"Ummm," she giggled. "I'm glad you know."

"What's up, Lucia?" I asked feeling on the verge of spitting in her face.

"I actually came over here to talk to you."

"Well talk."

"Well," she said swaying her hair. "I was wondering when we're going to meet this Blaze?"

"We?" I laughed. "Now who's checkin' for whose man?"

"Please believe, sweety," she smiled. "I'm not checkin' for your man. I'm actually happy to see you're doin' betta for yourself. You look kinda cute."

Cute? I thought. That's real funny. "Whateva," I responded letting her know that she didn't move me any which way. "Where's Marissa?" I continued slamming my locker shut.

"Here she comes now."

With that I dug into my purse which was hanging over my shoulder and secretly pressed the ring button on my new cell phone. I wanted it to sound off inside of my bag. Once I let it ring two times, I picked it up and looked at it as if someone was calling me. I was laying it on thick but this had to be a performance they'd never forget.

"Excuse me for a second, Lucia," I said pulling the phone out of my purse. "Blaze is calling me." With that I directed my attention to the phone that was off. "Hello?" I said lifting the phone to my ear. "Hey, baby! I miss you, too but you know I'm at school. I'll see you tonight. Ah Ha. Ah Ha." I was holding a full fledge conversation with myself and they didn't even know it. "Well I have to go, baby. I love you, too. Bye."

By the time I ended the call, Marissa was there. Before she said anything, Lucia pulled me to the side and said, "We're thinking about letting you in with the Strawberry Cuties. You still wanna be down?"

Already? I thought. I wanted to be a part of them so bad but I hadn't realized it would happen so soon. Besides, I still had three weeks worth of outfits to rock. I haven't even given the best of me yet. "Why now?" I asked.

"The girls think you'd be perfect."

"When did this happen?" I pried.

"It's been in the making for awhile," she advised. "Now if you don't want it, I'll let them know."

"Naw…naw!" I said stopping her with my hands from changing her mind. "I want it." I realize I probably sounded pressed but I didn't care. I didn't want her reneging on the offer.

"Well you gotta go through initiation first," she advised as Marissa looked at us a few steps away.

"Okay," I said trying to conceal the excitement. "When?"

"I'll let you know! But if you're not ready, you won't be getting in."

"I'll be ready."

She glanced at my ring and frowned. "Nice."

"I know."

When she walked off Marissa walked over to me.

"So what's that's all about?" She asked as she eyed my fit after watching her sister leave.

"She asked me to be in the Strawberry Cuties." I bragged.

"Are you serious?"

"Yes!"

For a minute she was excited for me until she realized my new status wouldn't include her.

"You not gonna fuck wit' me no more if you start hanging around wit' them."

"You my best friend," I said giving her a hug for the first time in a long time. "I wouldn't do you like that."

"What does that mean?" she asked as if she didn't believe me. "You been actin' like I didn't even exist lately."

"It's not like that! Blaze has been takin' a lot of my time," I told her. "And I'm gonna talk to Lucia. Don't worry."

"Talk to her about what?"

"Letting you in too."

"For real?" She said with raised eyebrows.

"Yep, and they'll let you in!"

"Alright, Kiante," she said taking a deep breath. "Anyway…what's up wit' this?" She asked lifting my hand up eyeing my ring.

"I told you," I said wiggling my hand in her face.

"Bitch, you were serious," she let out. "You really getting married?"

"You thought I was playin?" I asked as I hoped the bell wouldn't ring.   "Yeah,"   she said embarrassed that she doubted me. "I did. I mean…one minute you didn't have a man and the next you got a baller."

"Well, now you know when I say something, I mean it."

"When do I get to meet him?"

"Soon," I responded changing the subject. "We betta get to class before the bell ring though."

"Well does he have any friends?"

"I don't know," I said already knowing the answer. "But we'll see."

A MONOPOLY KIANTE

Marissa and I were standing in her living room looking crazy. We were expecting a call from Lucia and it seemed like it was taking forever. When it finally rang I stood up and grabbed the phone.

"Hey, Lucia!"

"Is that her?" Marissa asked tapping me on the arm.

I moved away from her because I didn't want Lucia knowing that we had been waiting on her call for over an hour. She was supposed to be giving us instructions on what we needed to do, to be accepted into the group.

"Sorry it took so long for me to call, but we're ready now. Meet us at the school in an hour." She sounded upbeat and suddenly I felt sure that whatever she wanted us to do, wouldn't be life threatening.

"No problem, Lucia! We're on our way now."

"And, Kiante...."

"Yes?" I asked hoping she wouldn't change her mind already.

"Bring Blaze."

Click.

Before I could tell her it wasn't possible, she hung up the phone. I stared at it for a second, debating on whether or not to call her back. I hadn't realized that my lies would bite me in the ass so soon. And now that it had, I wasn't sure what to do.

"What she say?!" Marissa responded her eyes too big for her face. I ignored her trying to get my thoughts together.

"She told us to come on."

"So why you look like that?" she questioned following me to the window.

"She wants me to bring Blaze."

"Well call him up!" She yelled grabbing her purse. "And let's go!"

"I can't call him up, Marissa. Give me a minute to think."

"Why not?!" She asked looking into my eyes.

Unable to face her, I sat on the couch. My plan backfiring had my nerves on edge and Marissa asking a million questions was not helping. It didn't make any sense to me that she'd want to see Blaze and because he wasn't real I didn't think to stop her. Before now, I had plans to tell everyone he was shot and killed. I would even come to school an emotional wreck...and now this.

"Sit down for a second, Marissa."

"I think I'll stand."

"Seriously! I have something to tell you. She sat down. "What is it?!"

It was time to come clean with Marissa but doing it was easier said then done. After how I treated her at school, and the way I'd been pretending to be too busy because I was with him, I knew she'd hold this against me forever. But if our getting into the group was based on them meeting Blaze, I knew we wasn't getting in.

"I lied, Marissa," I advised scooting next to her on the couch.

"Lied about what?" She asked.

I knew she couldn't hear me because I talked low on purpose, but it was difficult to tell her. "I said I lied." Again low, but louder than last time.

"About what?"

"About Blaze, Mari! He's not real."

"But...but...I don't understand."

"I got tired of people talking about me and how stupid I was for that thing that happened with Jamal in his basement. If I woulda known he'd tell everybody around school, I would never did that shit for him and his friends..."

"Hold up!" Marissa asked standing up. "You knew he had them in there and you still did it??"

Shit! My mouth moved so fast and now it was too late to stop it.

"I don't want to talk about that, Marissa. I'm trying to tell you I lied and I don't know what to do now."

While she was silent, I could tell she was remembering everything I told her. She was probably running around the things I told her about Blaze, and how Jamal had set me up. Her silence was killing me. I wanted to demand she say something, but thought better of it.

"Why you make him up? How come you told me all those things when he wasn't even real, Kiante? I'm supposed to be your best friend."

"Because it's embarrassing," I responded loud at first and then lower. I didn't want Mamma Maria hearing me in her room. "If I told you I made up a fake boyfriend, what would you have said to me?"

"I'da said get me one, too!" She responded. I couldn't help but giggle a little. "I'm your friend, Kiante, and what you did was fucked up…and don't think I'm letting you off the hook for the way you been acting…but you're still my friend."

"You think I'm crazy don't you?"

"Not really," she smiled. "I have to give you your props. You had the whole school talking about your new boyfriend. This one girl said she saw you with him at the IHOP."

"You lying?!" I erupted in laughter.

"How she gonna look when she find out he's not even real?" She giggled.

I was silent as she brought me to the realization that my secret would now be out. I was hoping that there was a way around it, but after her response, I was starting to doubt it.

"You think everybody will find out?" I asked.

"I don't know. I mean…you even had Crystal's fake ass fooled."

"So now what?" Her understanding gave me the permission to rely on her for help, because after Lucia's request, I was fresh out of ideas.

"We should still go," she advised. "She wanted to belong to the Strawberry Cuties just as bad as I did.

"And what should I say when she asks where's Blaze?"

"Tell her he couldn't come. Shit," Marissa responded placing her hands on her hips and swinging her hair. "Blaze ain't got time for this shit. That man's about makin' paper not about hangin' around no high school chicks."

I laughed when I heard how convincing she sounded, and for a moment, I forgot he wasn't real. So I followed her lead.

"Yeah, my man ain't got time for this shit," I added grabbing the keys to my car as we both walked out the door.

"And if she has any questions, I'll tell I saw him and he was fyyyne!"

We both laughed and I said, "They came to me I didn't come to them. So what I do with whoever is none of their business!"

It felt good the moment the words left my mouth, but I knew it wasn't how I really felt.

We made it to the school per Lucia's request and we were totally nervous. It was after school hours so nobody but the people who were in detention was inside.

"Where's Blaze?!" Lucia asked as we approached the bathrooms in the back of the school building where she told us to come. She was with the rest of the Strawberry Cuties.

"He couldn't make it on such short notice," I responded hoping that would be enough.

"Well why not?" She proceeded. "He don't care enough to show up for you?"

"Lucia, Blaze just got here from New York and he's handlin' bizness. He ain't got time to be comin' to no meeting at my school. If you wanna meet him you will, don't worry."

"That's sad you don't have your man in check," One of the members said.

"Yeah!" Raven added. "You would think how you be biggin' him up he'd show up for you."

"Well, you shouldn't be so worried about Kiante's man anyway, Raven," Marissa interjected.

"Maybe you should put more time into the one that got away from you."

"Fuck you, bitch!" Raven yelled.

"Don't even worry about it, girl," Karen said coming to her rescue.

I sat there in amazement that Lucia allowed them to talk to her sister like that. I was so disgusted that I even considered giving up on being a part of the crew. She could treat me as bad as she wanted to but Marissa was family. She was supposed to put them in check. But the more I tried to move or say something in Marissa's defense, I couldn't. I felt paralyzed all because I wanted to be popular and a part of their crew so badly.

"Marissa, why don't you go home?" Lucia asked.

"Because I want to do this too," she said readjusting her voice for her sister's comment. "And Kiante said she's not doing this without me."

"Is that true?" Lucia asked looking into my eyes.

"No," I said flatly.

All of them started laughing. I didn't care because there was no way I was letting Marissa ruin my chances. Besides I don't remember saying I'd do it without her. All I remember saying was I'd put in a good word for her and I did.

"Damn, Mari," Raven laughed. "Your friend leaving you hanging."

I could feel Marissa's eyes on the back of me but I remained turned toward them. For a while we stood in the hall eyeing one another, and I was starting to wonder again if betraying my friend and myself was worth all of this.

"I'm not leaving her hanging," I spoke up. "You didn't let me finish. I was gonna say there is *no* way I'm doing this without her. So are ya'll gonna continue to play games or are we gonna get down to it?"

Marissa smiled. "Yeah, what is the initiation?"

"Here's the thing," Lucia started looking briefly behind her at her friends before continuing for confirmation. "Unless you got Blaze, you can't get in."

"Yeah," Raven added. "So ya'll might as well turn around and come back when he cares enough about you."

As they started walking away, I turned around. Marissa's face was filled with disappointment and anger and it was my fault. Even though she didn't say it, I could tell she wanted to be a part of the Strawberry Cuties just as much as I did. I decided then to tell Lucia the truth. If it worked on Marissa, maybe Lucia would be just as understanding. And if not, I guess I ruined the chance at something I wanted ever since my freshman year at Ballou.

"Lucia, can I talk to you in private?" I asked walking up behind her. The rest of them stopped walking as I approached her. They all turned around to give us some privacy.

"Yeah, what's up?" She asked as we walked to the side of the hall out of earshot of everyone else.

"I have something to tell you."

"What is it?" She said breathing heavily.

"Blaze is not real and everything I did and said was a lie."

She frowned and stared at me in disbelief.

Silence.

"I'm soooo sorry, Lucia," I continued. "I just wanted to fit in and I knew you wouldn't accept me if I didn't make him up."

She looked at me as if she could spit in my face and instantly all the hopes I had of being in the group went out of the window. "So you played me?"

"NO!" I responded as the stinging in my nose reminded me that I was on the verge of crying. "I wasn't trying to play you. It wasn't even like that." I looked over at her crew and back at Lucia.

"Did Marissa know about this?" she asked glancing over at her.

"She just found out today."

"One last question…Is that ring fake?" she asked pointing to it.

I nodded my head yes. I didn't realize I was still wearing the biggest part of my shame on my finger.

"Only because I like you, we're still gonna put you through."

"For real?!" I was so excited I screamed and the moment I did, Marissa gave off a slight smile.

"Yep, for real." Although she was accepting us, she looked like something was heavily on her mind. I figured she was still angry with me for lying but I had all intentions of proving to her how bad I wanted to be down with the Strawberry Cuties. Whatever we had to do, I was going to do it. I just hope Marissa was too. "Follow me."

Everybody, including the eight other members of the club walked us into the girl's restroom. Once we were in, Marissa and I wondered how it applied to us getting into the group. But we quickly found out. Each member pushed open a stall door, so we could see the nasty toilets. Some of them were laughing and others just shook their heads in disgust.

"Come over here," Lucia demanded. We did as told. "Are you sure you want to be down? Cuz I don't want you wastin' my time, Kiante."

I nodded my head yes but Marissa didn't. She just stared at the toilets.

"Okay, ya'll gotta get on your knees, lift up the toilet seat, and lick around the bowls. If you do that, you're in."

I looked at Marissa who was shaking her head and frowning her face.

"And both of ya'll have to do it!" Lucia added looking at Marissa.

"I'm your fuckin' sister, bitch!" Marissa screamed approaching Lucia. "I can't believe you would ask me to lick a fuckin' toilet bowl."

I jumped in between both of them and used my hands to push both of them back. I knew if I didn't they would be rumbling as if the same blood didn't run through their veins.

"You're my sister at home, but out here," she giggled. "These are my sisters," she said pointing to the Strawberry Cuties. "So if you want it like you say you do, get on your fuckin' knees."

Without hesitation, Marissa broke out running. I ran after her almost breaking one of my heels. We were making too much noise to be in school after hours but I had to get through to her. The sound of her tennis shoes squeaking against the floor resonated. She was almost out the school's door when I reminded her I had the keys to the car by dangling them so that they made a clinking noise.

"I'm not trippin' off of that." She said eying them. "I'll walk before I do some shit like that!"

"Marissa," I said pushing her up against the lockers. "Why are you doing this to me?"

"Doing what?" she said knocking my hands off of her shoulders. "Why are you gonna do what she's asking you? Ever since you changed your hair, you've been acting differently. You're not even the same person. All you care about is fitting in to something that doesn't want you!"

"What are you talking about Marissa? You said you wanted this, too!"

"Kiante," she started as tears fell down her face. "Why are we staying here if they tellin' us we gotta lick some nasty ass toilet bowls to get in? In my mind," she said pointing at herself. "There ain't shit else to talk about cuz I'm not 'bout to stoop that low."

"Marissa, please," I begged, as the backed up tears finally fell down my face too. "Please don't leave! You heard what she said!"

"Oh what...that we both had to do it? Because at first you were willin' to do everything without me."

"That's not true, Marissa. It was me who told Lucia I wanted you in too."

"Listen, Kiante...and listen good...I'm not licking no fuckin' toilet bowl! I mean, I ain't lookin' for any special treatment, but my sister is losing her fuckin' mind. She treating me like I came off the street. I know for a fact that Raven and Karen didn't have to do something so nasty!"

"How you know what they had to do?"

"Because she's my sister."

"Well I know for a fact that Vanessa got punched in her face by every body in the group before she got in." I was lying again but so what. If she walked out of the door right now she took my chance at getting in the crew with her.

Marissa huffed and puffed before giving me answer. I waited anxiously holding my breath.

"What ya'll gonna do because we ain't got all day!" Lucia yelled coming into the hallway from the bathroom.

"We comin' now!" Marissa said wiping the tears from her face.

"Well hurry the fuck up before we change our mind and don't let you in!" She said disappearing into the bathroom.

When she was gone Marissa said, "I sure hope you'd do something like this for me."

"I would!" I said hugging her as if we weren't getting ready to slob down some pissy ass toilet bowls. "Thanks for not leaving me."

"Whateva!" She continued talking in her native language.

When we opened the door in the bathroom and watched them all holding their laughs, I pretended as if it didn't bother me. I told myself that they probably had to do something worse than this. Raven was on the phone telling somebody something and I'm sure it had to do with us.

I walked into one stall and Marissa walked into the other. All I saw was her knees hit the ground reluctantly one by one. I did the same, and prepared myself for the ultimate embarrassment.

After everything was done, I licked all eight bowls and it was truly the nastiest shit I ever experienced in my life.

I'd rather suck dirty Chris's dick four more times before doing this shit ever again. Even though it was hard for me, it was harder for Marissa. On the eighth bowl she was so disgusted, that she threw up inside it. But just like that, we were done. And for some reason I didn't care about doing it. All that concerned me was that it was over. The way I saw it, it was worth knowing that tomorrow, we would finally be official. And I would finally be popular.

FUCKED UP AGAIN
KIANTE

Marissa and I had just gotten to school. I looked cute wearing a pair of tight blue jeans and my Baby Phat blue jean jacket showing a little cleavage. I also threw on a pair of my black Via Spiga boots. Marissa wore a pair of jeans too and a white "T" that said, *Don't Blame Me.*

"When do we get our jackets?" I asked Marissa parking the car.

"I asked Lucia this morning and she said today," Marissa said fixing her hair. "All mouths gonna drop when we walk down the hall with them on."

"I know," I smiled. "We finally Strawberry Cuties! I bet you Jamal gonna really be on my shit now!"

We got out of the car and walked toward school and I noticed all eyes were on us. Marissa noticed Chris walking in our direction and called his name.

"Chris!" she smiled eager to tell him the 411 on us getting in the crew. But instead of walking over to her, he walked away.

"Girl, I think he just played you," I laughed.

"He must be jealous," she snickered. "Poor thang, the word must be out already," Marissa continued finally noticing the stares.

"I guess so," I laughed. When I realized I left my purse in my car, I stopped. "Shit! I left my bag in the car."

"Want me to go with you?" she asked.

"No," I said jogging. "You go get our jackets from Lucia. I'll be back in a minute."

When went to my car, I got my purse out of my backseat and headed back to the building. That's when, I noticed people laughing. I wondered what was so funny. But the moment I hit the doors and walked inside the school I knew exactly what was up.

I quickly discovered that Raven wasn't on the phone yesterday when we were in the bathroom. That bitch was taking pictures on it because I saw everyone holding pictures printed out on paper of us licking the toilets. I am devastated!

My steps slowed up. At one time the hallway seemed so short and now it seemed so long. How could she do this to me? To us.

"Damn, Kiante," Crystal said coming out of nowhere. "Mr. Jenkins would've cleaned the toilets. You didn't have to do it with your mouth. Ugggghh."

Everyone erupted in laughter. People were pointing and laughing. Their fingers felt as if they were poking me. I felt like kicking Raven's ass but that would mean walking past everyone to get to her and I couldn't do it. But where was Marissa? There was no way she couldn't see this. Somehow I made it to my locker and when I did, I gasped. Raven had written, *Blaze was fake*, in red marker. I turned around looking for her. I decided to kick her ass right there! Suddenly I saw someone running up to me. It was Marissa.

"I can't stay here!" she cried. "Just give me the keys," she responded. "I'm gonna stay in the car!"

I pulled them out of my pocket and she snatched them from me and bolted out of the door. One thing was certain, neither one of us would be finishing out the rest of the day at school. I should've known something was up when Marissa called Chris's whack ass, and he walked in the other direction, but we had no idea the lengths Lucia would go through to destroy our lives. And for what?!

Once I made it outside the sunshine blinded me as I attempted to look for Marissa. When I saw her at the car, I walked toward it but was stopped short by Hempay. He was calling me but there was no way I could face him. This was beyond any embarrassment I could have ever have imagined. I decided to ignore him and walk toward my car. But he ran behind me finally catching me a few feet away from my ride. Grabbing me on my upper right arm he pulled me toward him.

"What do you want, Hempay?!" I yelled snatching my arm away from him. "I have to go!"

"I want to talk to you!" He said irritated by my response. "You heard me calling you back there? Why you keep runnin'?"

"What difference does it make, Hempay?! I'm a fake okay! And everybody in there knows it!"

"I don't know why you trippin' off that stupid shit! You betta then them bitches anyway."

"Stop playing games! What do you want? To tell me how stupid I was for letting them trick me?" I paused only briefly giving him no chance to answer. "Well if that's what the fuck you want to do don't worry about it! I already know." I tried to make it to my car but again he grabbed me.

"Don't fuckin' leave! Just let me talk to you for a sec," he pleaded.

I threw my hands in the air wishing he'd leave me alone. I looked at Marissa inside the car crying and I wished I was in there with her. Usually at this time everybody would be going to first period but instead everyone stood in the background, watching me and Hempay standing in the student parking lot.

"You're not stupid," he sounded serious and compassionate at the same time. "What them bitches did back there was fucked up! And you shouldn't be out here beating yourself up about it!"

Bitch? I was surprised he used that word to describe his girlfriend.

"You need to be standing up for yourself and showin' them you got heart!" he continued.

"I just want to go home, Hempay. Anyway you need to stop acting like you give a fuck about me because I know you don't. You made that clear the other night, remember?"

"If I ain't give a fuck," he said reaching for my hand. "Why would I be out here? Huh?!" His words were hard but the meaning was gentle and I immediately wanted to fall into his arms. But I didn't.

"I gotta go, Hempay! I'm sorry! Bye!"

I pulled myself away from him and jumped into my car. As I sped off, I could see him standing in the same spot we shared just moments ago. He didn't move until I was almost completely out of sight.

"Are you okay?" I asked looking at Marissa and then back at the road. She could barely speak but managed to nod that she was okay. She was crying so hard that at first I started to take her to the hospital. Over and over she kept saying "Why? Why! Why?!" Unfortunately I didn't have any answers for her, because I didn't know either.

CHANCE TO APOLOGIZE

KIANTE

I sat on my bed in the dark talking to Lucia on the phone. My window was open and the night air pushed my navy blue curtains open allowing the moonlight to shine on my face.

I had finally managed to get a hold of Lucia because I had called her several times on her cell phone and each time it went straight to voicemail. I wanted answers and I knew only she could be the one to give them to me. The moment I reached her I heard my parents coming into the house from outdoors. I reduced my voice to conceal the conversation I was having with my suppose-to-be friend.

"Hello," I said shocked she answered the phone.

"Yes."

"Lucia! Why did you do that today at school?"

"Do what?" she giggled. "You did that to yourself. I wasn't the one on my hands and knees licking toilet bowls."

Lucia was treating what she did as if it was a joke and I didn't see shit funny.

"So it's okay to take pictures of me and Marissa and pass them out at school? You looked bad too you know."

"Listen to you," she laughed. "You're crying about something that happed hours ago."

"It may be hours ago to you but Marissa is still upset and I'm sitting here stuck. I thought you were my friend!"

"I never said that."

"You're gonna get what you deserve, Lucia! Watch!"

"Is everything okay, Kiante?" My mother asked as she opened my door unannounced. I could see my father standing behind her awaiting my answer too.

"Yes, mommy. I'm just talking to Lucia that's all."

"Ya'll are not fighting are you? You've been friends too long."

I loved my mother and father but sometimes they had a tendency to get into my business. I didn't ask them who they were talking to on the phone so why were they asking me?

"Can I be alone?" I answered. "This is kinda important."

"Alright, honey," my father said looking at my mother. "We'll be out here if you need us."

"I know, daddy."

"Are you still going with me and your mother to the site tomorrow for the unveiling? We're almost finished with the construction for the daycare center and I'd like everybody on the job to meet my beautiful little girl." He said.

I forgot I told him I'd go. Honestly I wasn't in the mood to see anybody tonight or tomorrow. But if I didn't go, I knew he'd really suspect something was up in my life. Lately I'd been incognito. Plus he'd been working day and night on that job for two months. He was proud of it and wanted to share it with us.

"Okay, daddy," I responded hoping Lucia wouldn't hang up. "I'll go."

He smiled and said, "Alright, baby. We have to be up early. Someone vandalized the front of the building so we have to remove it with some industrial paint remover."

"Alright, daddy," I said trying to wrap it up. "Good night."

"Good night, sweetheart," he said.

"Good night, baby," my mother added.

When they closed the door and I said hello...Lucia was gone. That didn't do anything but irritate me even more. But finally, I knew exactly how I'd be getting back at her. She deserved everything she had coming.

THE DRAMA BEGINS

KIANTE

"What are you doing in here, Kiante?" Marissa asked me as I walked into her room. "I want to be by myself right now."

"Trust me," I told her as I sat on her bed. "I wanted to be alone, too. But my father dragged me out of the house today."

"So what's up, Kiante? Cuz I know you didn't come all the way out here to tell me about your day."

"You're right. But what I came over here for, I think will make both of us feel better."

"What you gonna do? Reverse everything that happened yesterday? Because that's the only thing that will work for me," she said as she threw the covers over her head and curled up into a ball.

"I can't reverse everything, but I can get the next best thing for us...revenge."

"What are you talkin' about?!"

"Don't you think she should pay for what the fuck she did to us?" I whispered.

"All I want to do is sleep."

"You'll have plenty of time for that," I responded yanking the covers off her head. I didn't realize she was under there damn near naked. I told her to put some clothes on when I was mooned by a red thong and yellow titties.

"Listen you came over here," she said laughing slightly. "So what's your plan anyway?" She snatched the covers from me and hid herself.

"Look what I got!" I said as I showed her the metal container in a plastic bag on the floor.

"What is it?" she questioned stealing a quick look at it. "Because for real, I'm not in the mood to be playing guessing games right now."

Before telling her my plan, I decided to apologize for what happened. I realized that had it not been for me, we wouldn't be in this situation. Still, what Lucia did was wrong and the way she acted showed me how she was trying to treat me.

"I'm sorry, Marissa. I know you're mad at me, and you have every right to be. But trust me," I said on my knees while she lie on the bed. "After we do this, I'll never ask you to do anything else."

"What is it?" she asked sitting up in the bed showing the first signs of life.

"I have the perfect get back. Especially after I called her yesterday and she said we both got what we deserved."

"You talked to my sister?" she asked looking at me confused. "She hasn't said two words to me."

"Yeah...I did," I advised. "She told me she didn't care about you and that she could never stand you stand you to begin with. She's tired of you trying to be like her. That was the reason she did everything."

I lied to her but I needed her buy-in. Later I'd make it up to her.

"I hate her," she said. I could see she was on the verge of crying. I knew I had to stop her quickly.

"Don't let her upset you. She'll be getting everything she has coming to her soon."

"I thought she did what she did because of you."

"Me?" I questioned.

"Yeah. I thought she did it because she's jealous of you."

"She told you that?"

"Naw," she said looking at me as if I was stupid. "You know she would never admit anything like that to me. I heard her talking to Raven and Karen about how you act when Hempay's around. She think something's up with that."

"What?!" I yelled. "Why she say that? Hempay wouldn't think about me when he has someone as pretty as Lucia on his arm."

"Hempay, stays talking about you, Kiante. Every other thing out of his mouth was about you and Blaze before everybody found out he wasn't real. He was *way* too concerned with you fucking with him. I think they broke up cause of that shit, too!"

"They broke up?"

"Yep." She responded. That explained why he called her a bitch outside. Here he was, worried about what I was doing, and he was messing with the baddest girl in school.

"But fuck that shit," she said waking me out of my daydreams. "What you got planned, cuz I'm down wit' that shit now."

Walking to the plastic bag I brought in, I was careful not to maneuver its contents. Because what I was holding was strong enough to fuck up everything in this room, including us.

"What's that?" She asked pointing at the can.

I locked her bedroom door and whispered, "Acid and two pairs of rubber gloves."

"Where the fuck you get acid from?! And betta yet, why is it here?!" She asked as she stood straight up moving away from it.

"You know my daddy's in construction. So he's got all kinda stuff like this lying around. I stole some out of his work truck when I went to his job today."

"How you get it out?"

"It wasn't easy. I had to ask a million questions just so he'd show me where it was. I wanted to know where he kept this, and where he kept that. He was so busy liking the fact that I was asking questions about what he did for a living that he didn't suspect anything. So when everything was over, I lost him, turned back around and stole one of the cans."

"What's your plan with it?" Marissa questioned.

"We gonna throw it on Lucia's car," I responded rubbing my hands together. "It'll fuck her pretty little paint job right up!"

I just knew she was gonna say no, but instead she said, "You lied."

"Huh?"

"You told me you couldn't reverse that shit she did to us. This is way better!" She said cheering me on.

"I knew you'd feel me on this."

"Let's do it!"

"Serious?!" I asked hoping she wouldn't say no.

"Yes! Let's do it and quick before I change my mind."

"Okay…but let me go out there first to make sure nobody bothers us."

I returned in five minutes and she was fully dressed and ready to go…Where I don't know.

"Nobody is checking for us out in the living room. We good."

After we put the rubber gloves on, I quietly as possible opened the window.

"What you doin'?!" She asked.

"What does it look like? I'm opening the window."

"I see that but why?"

"First of all a keep your voice down, Marissa! Somebody's gonna hear your ass!"

"Alright," she said lowering her voice a little. "But why are you opening the window? I thought we were goin' downstairs to do it."

"No we're not," I said shaking my head before pushing her shoulders down on the bed while I sat in a chair across from her. As I looked at her, she kept her eyes on the acid making sure it didn't fall over. "If we go downstairs, whoever's in the living room will see us with this can and it'll look suspicious."

"So you wanna pour it out of the window?"

"Yes!" I said excitedly. "It's perfect."

"What about your car?" she asked standing up to look out of the window. "Did you move it?"

"Yes. It's in the front."

"You don't think that's a little suspicious since you never park around front?!"

"Nope!"

"Well I do," she said as if she was trying to back out. "Maybe we shouldn't do it tonight."

"Well I think we should! All I know is this," I said taking a deep breath. "What Lucia did yesterday was wrong, and she gotta pay for it. *Tonight*! I'm tired of being the nice girl! People have been pushing me ova for too long!"

"This seems a little too brutal, Kiante."

"And what she did yesterday wasn't?" I challenged.

Taking a deep breath she said, "Aigh't."

I didn't bother asking her if she was ready because *ready* or not, *we* were doing it now! With the window already opened, Marissa carefully held the can in her hands. But as if a volcano was erupting up under her, she started shaking. "Calm down," I said real softly placing my hand on the can. "We don't want this stuff falling all over us."

"I'm tryin'," she said real low as if talking too loud would shake it too.

"When I say the coast is clear, pour it outside. Her car is right up under the window so it's perfect. It should fall right on it."

She nodded her head okay.

After sticking my head outside, I made sure nobody was looking. "The coast is clear. Do it now."

With that she poured the acid out of the window and as she was doing it, I saw a figure appear out of the back door next to Lucia's car. Instead of getting the car, the acid fell out of the can and onto the person. The scream was so deafening, that we both were petrified when we heard it. Marissa dropped the empty canister on the floor and we slammed the window shut. Remnants of the acid spilled on the floor and we both watched it eat at the rug. I could only imagine what it had done to the stranger's body.

"OH shit!" Marissa said as we sat up under the window. She instantly started crying. Her reaction caused me to be more on edge. "Who do you think that was?"

"I don't know," I said shaking my head. The cries of the person became clearer and louder. Thoughts of the pain they were in ran through my mind.

"Mami! Marissa! Help me! Please!" the voice cried outside.

"Oh my God, Kiante!" Marissa said with wide eyes. "That sounds like Lucia's voice!"

I looked at her and then down at the carpet wondering what fate held for us. The more I thought about it, the more scared I became.

IN THE HOSPITAL
KIANTE

The hospital felt hot as we wondered what would happen next. And although I was trying to remain calm, Marissa was totally losing it at the moment.

"Marissa, calm down!" I told her gripping both of her shoulders tightly. "If you don't stop crying, they'll know we had something to do with it!"

My eyes quickly scanned the waiting room and for a second, I was happy everyone was occupied with how Lucia was doing. Mamma Maria was an emotional wreck and Hempay was there to console her. J.D was there at first but when he realized Mamma Maria relied on Hempay for support, he left the hospital in a jealous rage. Too much was happening too soon.

"What are you talkin' about, Kiante? My sister's in a hospital bed fighting for her life. Why wouldn't I cry?"

"I'm upset, too! But you don't see me crying now do you? We have to remain calm. You have to pull yourself together."

"If crying makes them think we had something to do with it, they already know," she cried her face beet red and wet with tears.

"That's not true. They don't know yet. The only way they will is if you act like it or tell them. You don't plan on telling them do you?"

"I can't do this, Kiante. I can't keep a secret like this to myself."

My stomach churned and I felt heavy. "You're not keeping it by yourself. I know too. We have each other!"

"Did you see her face, Kiante? She doesn't look anything like my beautiful sister anymore. Did you see what we did to her? And for what? Putting pictures in lockers at school?"

"I seen her face. But you know what?" I paused. "She deserved it. If she hadn't did what she did to us, none of this woulda happened."

Marissa frowned at me and shook her head. "That's my sister, Kiante!"

"I know who she is!" I yelled back, hoping no one overheard us. "But have you forgotten how we felt yesterday? Besides, it was an accident. I'm sure she'll be okay."

"Accident or not it was still our fault! I got to tell somebody," she continued as she got up and walked toward everyone waiting to get news on Lucia's condition.

I grabbed her again and pushed her up against the wall. The edge of a picture frame of the hospital map pressed up against the back of her head.

"Get off me, bitch!"

"No! Not until you listen!" I yelled a little louder than I wanted to. I removed my hands from her right before Mamma Maria saw me. "Now sit down."

She stared at me and put her hands on her hips as if I couldn't tell her anything.

"Mari, sit down. Please."

She regretfully complied. "Now listen," I said attempting to take a different approach. "If you don't calm down, both of us will get into trouble."

"But I'm scared!"

"I know, Mari. I am too. But somebody has to have a leveled head. And for real, we got to think about ourselves now."

"Who are you?" she asked looking at me as if she didn't now me.

"What are you talkin' about?"

"I asked who are you? Lately you've been acting like you don't care about anybody but yourself."

What was wrong with this bitch?! If I got out of this okay, and without getting into trouble, I made a promise to myself to at some point cut her ass off. I'm trying to protect her and I and she's fucking ungrateful. Besides this wasn't just my fault, it was ours.

Before I responded I glanced over and saw Hempay now alone and sitting in a chair a few over from ours. His fine black hair was neatly cornrowed and his face was in his palms. Although I couldn't see his tears, I could tell he was silently crying and it hurt me that Lucia was because of it.

"Kiante! Are you listening to me?" She asked breaking me out of my thought process.

"I hear what you're saying and you're right. If you truly feel guilty or that I'm acting like I don't care, I'll prove to you that, it isn't true," I continued reaching into my purse. "Let's put an end to all of this right now."

"What are you doing?" she asked wiping the tears and eyeing the wireless phone I removed from my purse and held in my hand.

"I'm calling the police so that they can come down here and take a report."

"What?"

"Well you said you wanted to tell somebody, we might as well get it over with. You heard the detective say earlier when he took our reports that they didn't have a suspect." The police questioned everybody in the building after Lucia was burned. "We might as well tell him not to look any further," I said pretending I was dialing numbers. "I just hope Mamma Maria can handle this. It will probably break her heart that her own daughter was involved."

"Don't' do that!" she screamed causing Hempay to look at us briefly for a minute. "Please." She lowered her voice.

"Why?" I said placing the turned off phone to my ear. "This is what you wanted."

Marissa glanced down the hall and saw her mother broken down, hurt and in pain. She was standing up by the emergency curtain watching the doctor's work diligently to save what was left of her face. She knew there was no way she could walk over to her mother and tell her she was partially to blame for everything.

"I hate you!" she finally said. "I wished I never listened to you."

"I didn't twist your arm," I reminded her.

"I'm not going to hurt my mother, but I will never forget this," she responded before standing up and joining her mother.

Suddenly I could care less about how she felt. I wasn't going to jail for anybody. Instead of going behind her, I decided to sit next to Hempay. He needed me the most and in my mind, it was high time we made up.

6 YEARS LATER

*C*hemistry *was crazy from the get-go and nei-*
ther one of us knew why. We didn't build
nothing overnight Cuz a love like this takes
some time. People swore it off as a phase. Said we
can't see that! Now from top to bottom! They see
that we did that! (yes) It's so true that (yes) We've
been through it (yes) We got real shit (yes) See ba-
by we been...Too strong for too long! And I can't be
without you baby! And I'll be waiting up until you
get home...

That is my mothafuckin song! Mary J. stay
bringin' them hits! Me and her are alike in more
ways than one. She went through some shit and
now she's in love, and I went through some shit and
now I'm in love. If you would've told me that at 23
years old, I would be a married woman, with a
beautiful four year old little girl and a successful
business, I would've called you a liar. But I have a
sleuth of good friends, a handsome husband and a

wonderful little girl. Life for me is better than I could ever have imagined, in fact it is the bomb!

I was blasting my music when I heard my phone ring in my red 2006 Mercedes Benz E320. I smiled the moment I saw the word "Husband" with his face flash across my phone's screen.

"Yes, honey," I smiled pushing the button for the speaker. "Did Laila get out okay for school today? Cuz I wouldn't let her carry that IPOD to school just so she can listen to the JoJo CD for the fiftieth time." My daughter loved that white girl more than she loved herself.

"Baby." His voice straight, quick and to the point.

"Yes, honey," I said looking at the phone and than back at the road. His attitude was different and immediately I knew something was wrong. "Is everything okay, baby?!"

"I need you to turn around and come home." Is this a death call?! I thought. Did something happen to my parents?! I hated that he wouldn't tell me more. Leaving me hanging was worse than not knowing.

"What is it, Hempay?!" I hated yelling at him but we've been together for over five years and married for four. He should know how I feel about being held in suspense.

"I don't want you to get into an accident, Kiante!" His voice reminded me who was in charge so I backed down a little. And only a little. "So come home, and I'll tell you everything you need to know. Just so you know," he continued. "Nothing has happened to Laila or your parents so don't worry about that. So drive safe but hurry up."

"Alright," I said ending the call.

After he confirmed for me that my family was okay, I exhaled. If something happened to my family I'd lose my mind. The next call I made was to one of my best friends. Since I had to go home, I couldn't meet up with them.

"Raven, don't go down to the store this morning. I'll bring the shoes I got for you and Karen later on tonight," I told her from my cell phone.

"Why what's wrong? Did Hempay's ass hate again?! You know he can't stand me."

"Hempay likes you. It's just that every time we're together, I come home late or some bullshit like that."

"Then why you not going to work?" she asked prying into my business as usual.

"Hempay called and told me to come back home. He said he needed to talk to me." I explained.

"Is whatever he has to tell you that bad where it can't wait until after you meet with me?"

"He didn't tell me." I sighed. "But he is my husband."

"Well I have to tell you something. So make sure you call me back."

"Ah Ahn, bitch! Tell me now."

"Nope. I wanna make sure you comin' to see me! I was gonna wear those shoes tonight and everything."

"I'm gonna give them to you, Raven" I said trying to convince her. The truth was I didn't know if I'd be able to come back out or not later after hearing the way Hempay sounded. "But you know I can't stand when you say you have to tell me something and then don't. Now tell me what's up."

"Okay," she said her voice slightly muffled as if she was pressing her face against the phone. "You remember Rico right?"

"Yeah I remember his ass! I still got the scratches on my pussy from when his friend fingered my ass."

"That's your fault, Kiante," she said. "I'm not the one who was trying to play little miss nice girl. Anyway, if you'da let him hit that ass instead of eating your pussy and fingering you while he jacked off, you would not have gotten bruised." She laughed.

"You know, Hem pay's the only one I give this pussy too. I don't cheat unlike your fast ass."

"News flash!" she said smacking her tongue. "Letting another man eat your pussy and finger you is cheating."

"Not in my book," I advised.

"Enough about you," she responded skipping the subject. "Why Rico tell me last night he wanted to try something different."

I know it was fucked up that we were keeping time with the same dude but that's how we rolled. We held each other's secrets till death.

"*Okay...*" I said as I turned the corner for my street. "What's so wrong with wanting to try something different?"

"What's wrong with it is he pulled out my dildoe and wanted me to put it in his ass while he was fucking me."

"Uuuuuggghhh! Please tell me you're playing!"

"I'm not," she whispered. "He came and everything. Hard too!"

"What the fuck?! Are you still with him now?"

"Girl his ass is right here snoring. I'm done with him, Kiante. That's no lie."

"You need to be. There's nothing manly about a nigga who likes it in the ass. I'm sorry."

"You already telling me what I know."

"I just hope you're listening."

"I am. But look, I gotta go," Raven said as her voice got a little louder. "Don't forget to bring my shoes tonight. Or I'm not fuckin' wit' you know more."

"Alright, Raven. Later."

Now I had to see her later because she had a tendency to hold grudges forever. Me, Raven and Karen became good friends ever since I eventually made it into the Strawberry Cuties. It started with me inviting the girls over to my house, to buy Lucia something nice while she was in the hospital. We held conversations, realized we liked the same boys and hand similar dreams. After awhile, it seemed like we were sisters more than friends. From then on, they saw how cool I was and I just fit in. Just like me, both of them got degrees and were running successful businesses.

I owned a Starbucks franchise off of Brinkley road in Maryland and my girls were part owners of a Marketing Firm called, Water Diamonds. We had sexy luxurious lives and the money to go with it. I had a nice cozy home in Potomac Maryland and Raven and Karen were able to purchase property in Windy Springs, the same development me and Hempay lived in. We attended elite parties and surrounded ourselves with like-minded people so our money could continue to roll in. We knew that if you wanted to make money, you had to hang around people with money.

On top of all that, we stay in the gym so our bodies were toned and perfect. We talked all the time about women who put no time into their bodies and wondered why their men got snatched. It wasn't happening to us! Trust and believe! The way I think about it is, when you surround yourself with people who like to grind like you, the money continues to roll in. But if you hang around bums, you lie with them.

Surrounding yourself around people who don't aspire to do shit, ain't doin' nothing but bringing you down with them. What does that mean? *Well,* for me it means I'd cut off anybody who wasn't on my level. Including old acquaintances. I'm what people call the epitome of beauty, money and power and no one had to tell me because I already knew it.

When I pulled up into my three-car driveway, I noticed the door of my husband's black 2006 Hummer H3 was open. The neighborhood was extremely safe but I was still worried. I hit the button to the electric driveway, eyeing his car door periodically as I parked my car. When my feet hit the concrete I realized I didn't have on shoes. I almost always kicked them off when I was driving. It felt comfortable to me. Reaching back into the car, I grabbed my black sleep pumps that I recently purchased from Saks and slid into them. Then I pulled out my pink Marc Jacob bag and hit my alarm.

Once out of the car, I walked to his truck, glanced inside to make sure everything was okay. When I saw that it was, I carefully closed the door. It was strange that it was open because Hempay loved his truck almost as much as he loved me and our daughter. If he left it open and didn't have time to close it, I was positive that something had definitely gone wrong.

After putting my keys in my double glass stain door, and pushing my way inside our home, my daughter ran over to me damn near knocking me to the floor. Whatever's going on it couldn't be that unpleasant because it hadn't affected Laila's mood one bit.

"Mommy! Mommy! Mommy!" She yelled jumping up and down. "I miss you!"

"You did," I said in the high pitched voice I often used when talking to her. "I missed you, too. But you just seen me about an hour ago."

Had I known I could've received this much love from a human being, I would've had her a long time ago. It was because of Laila that Hempay placed the ring on my finger. For years he felt guilty about what happened to Lucia and how he left her side to be with me. But after Laila was born, he couldn't deny the fact that he loved me. My parents were worried at first that I wouldn't get my degree from Howard University when I got pregnant with her, but rested easy when they saw me finally walk across the stage.

"I see you got a free day out of school, young lady," I said hugging her after placing my keys on the door table. "Muah! Muah! Muah!" I loved bombarding her with kisses. Her dark beautiful skin and shiny black hair resembled her father's so much that it was un-real. I joked with him all the time that if he was a girl, he'd look just like Laila. After laying it on thick with Laila, my eyes roamed around our home searching for my husband.

When I didn't see him in the front area, I kicked off my shoes, picked up my purse and walked toward the dining area almost knocking over Sarah. "Good morning, Mrs. Carey. Your husband is waiting for you in his study. I'll make Laila breakfast. Do you want anything?"

"Yes. I smiled. "Please bring both of us coffee and some croissants."

"Right away, Mrs. Carey."

"Thanks, Sarah." I said handing her my purse. "And make sure you bring me extra sugar, too. You know I hate strong tasting coffee."

"Right away, Mrs. Carey," she said again.

As I nervously adjusted my graphite chiffon tunic dress with the grey slip by Peter Som under it, I realized how scared I really was to hear whatever news he had for me. I only frantically adjusted my clothing if I was worried, and right now I was. Whatever my husband had to tell me was so serious, that he didn't bother going to one of the three barber shops he owned. My only hope was that he didn't find out that every now and again I acted up when I was with Raven or Karen, by fucking around with other dudes on the side.

When I reached his study, the door was open and I could see his framed degree on the wall. He received it from the University of the District of Columbia. I begged him to go to Howard with me but he insisted on being around the few thugs he grew up with who decided to go to college. Most of them are back on the street, degrees and all. Hempay's the only one who's running a legitimate business but he has the nerve to talk about my friends. Just because he remembers how mean they were to me when we were in high school. So the fuck what! Shit changes, people change and I finally have the life I always wanted.

"Mommy, Sarah wants me to eat! I'm not hungry!" My daughter yelled stopping me from walking into his office.

Hempay appeared on cue and interjected before I could answer. Stooping to her level he said, "Baby, mommy and daddy have a lot to talk about. Now you go in there and let Sarah feed you. After that I want you to work on the workbooks in your room."

"Daddy!" she whined. "I don't want to."

"Laila," he said dropping his voice the way my father use to do with me. "Did you hear what I said?"

"Yes," she said hanging her head.

"Now go."

When she was out of sight he led me into his study. He was more serious about Laila's schooling than I was. He did her homework with her every night and most of the time I was out of the loop with what was going on with her. I can't count the number of times he's gone off on a teacher for what he called, *Not Taking the Proper Interest in her Education.*

When we were alone, he wrapped his arms around me and tenderly rubbed my back. I couldn't return his affections because my arms were down against my sides. His body had gotten more muscular over the years due to working out. When he let me go and looked into my eyes, I knew something was wrong and he was having trouble telling it to me. I just wished he stopped beating around the bush and got to the fucking point.

"You left your truck door open." I said trying to break the ice.

"Oh," he said taking a deep breath. "Did you close it for me?"

"Yes."

"After getting the call on my phone I forgot to close it."

"I knew if you did that something was definitely up."

"I know," he smiled. "That's not something I do. So if you ever see it again, just know that something's really wrong."

"Well," I said even more nervous than to begin with. "Are you gonna tell me what's going on?"

"Sit down, baby," he said as he sat on the edge of his mahogany desk, while I sat in front of him. "Baby, something terrible has happened."

How stupid does he think I am? I know something happened otherwise I would be at work smelling coffee instead of looking at him sitting on the edge of his desk beating around the bush.

"Hempay, please tell me what's going on! I'm so scared right now I can shit on myself! Be real with me. Tell me what's going on. I can handle it!"

He stood up and gently rubbed his hand down the side of my face. I leaned into it and he said, "Marissa's dead."

I jumped up, accidentally knocking the expensive office chair back fracturing the leg on impact. "Hempay," I said breathing heavily. "What do you mean Marissa's dead?"

"Her mother came home early and she hadn't heard from her all day. When she called her for dinner she wouldn't answer and when she told her she got a phone call she didn't pick up the line in her room."

"Why couldn't she just open the door?"

"It was locked, Kiante. But in the morning when she heard her alarm go off without being stopped she had J.D kick it in and found her dead."

I covered my mouth. "Oh my God!"

"Once they got in, they found a note by her bed. She slit her wrists," He continued picking up the broken chair and placing it up against the wall. He didn't say it right then but I knew he was upset that he spent so much money for something that broke in one second. "The funeral's this weekend."

"I can't go," I said shaking my head. "I can't do it."

"Baby, you have to," he said as he rapidly stroked my shoulders and arms. "Ya'll grew up together. And before Lucia's accident, you were best friends. You know you can't do that shit. You have to go to the funeral."

"I can't believe she actually killed herself. I mean, she been telling me she would ever since Lucia got burned in that accident, but I never thought she'd actually go through with it. It doesn't make any sense."

"Why would she want to kill herself? It wasn't her fault."

"I know, baby. But she still hated seeing her like that."

Because Marissa and I kept it a secret that we had everything to do with what happened to Lucia, I couldn't tell Hempay but so much. He didn't know about the many nights I stayed on the phone begging her not to tell what happened knowing that at any moment, she could break the silence. As long as I lived, I planned to keep it that way. And a part of me was glad she was dead.

"Here is your coffee," Sarah said as she entered the room.

"Next time knock!" I snapped at her.

"Sorry, Mrs. Carey."

"It's okay, Sarah," Hempay responded looking at me. "You can leave us alone now."

He gave me the look he always did when he felt I was too hard on Sarah. She quickly placed the coffee on the table and ran out. Hempay walked me over to his leather sofa and grabbed my favorite red cup filled to the brim with coffee and handed it to me. You'd think by now I'd be tired of coffee since I own a Starbucks, but I never was. The moment the French Vanilla aroma tickled my nose I felt partially relaxed.

Sipping the coffee I leaned back into the sofa. There was no way I could see myself going to that funeral. But before I could build up the nerve to say anything to Hempay, he landed a passionate kiss on my lips. His eyes were always closed when he kissed me, but as dumb as it looked to bystanders I always kept mine open. I loved looking at his face and the way we looked when our lips met. He was more handsome than any man I'd ever thought I'd get in my life.

"I love you, baby. And I don't want you worrying yourself about anything," he paused as his voice deepened but remained gentle. "But you have to go to that funeral. Maria was good peoples to you and me. We owe her the respect of going to her youngest daughter's funeral."

"Let me think about it."

"Aight. But you *are* going. There are a lot of people who are going to be expecting you to be there."

When he said that, suddenly the only thought on my mind about Marissa's funeral was what I'd be wearing. He was right. Everyone would be looking at the new me and many of them I hadn't seen since I left high school. After me and Hempay graduated from high school, there was no reason to go back. But contemplating the look on their faces helped me make my decision about going to the funeral. I was sure a lot of people from school would be there since they never moved. Oh well...I guess I'm going after all.

IN THE BEDROOM

W hen I stepped into my bedroom the scented candles were sweet to my nose. The lights were dim and although I know my husband was in there waiting on me, I was still anxious. I went over Raven's to give her the shoes I picked up for her, and afterwards we went shopping for something to wear to the funeral. We both knew it was imperative to go in looking nothing less than flawless to represent our lives together.

Without seeing him, suddenly music came from the Bose wall unit. Finally he appeared from the bathroom. His chocolate covered skin was slightly bronzed due to standing out side for hours washing our cars. His hair was pulled back in the silky ponytail and he was wearing nothing but a pair of new white Polo boxers. His muscular body looked inviting and I could no longer wait for him to hold me in his arms.

"Get over here," he said reaching out for me.

Without hesitation, I fell into his arms and inhaled the Burberry cologne he wore.

"Ummmmm," I moaned. "What's all this for?"

"Cuz I don't want you worrying about everything. I need you to know that I got you and I love you more than anything."

"I know, baby," I giggled.

"I know you know it," he responded looking into my eyes. "But I need you to feel it. There is nothing more I ever wanted than for you to be my wife."

With that he fell into me and pressed his juicy thick lips onto mine. The fresh taste of toothpaste lingered within his kiss. His hands gripped my body as he pulled me closer and I couldn't move anymore. With passionate strokes, he worked his way from the top of my back down to the middle. But his lips never left mine.

As if I was on the ride of my life, he suddenly lifted me off my feet and carried me to the bed. I've seen our cherry wood platform bed many times but tonight it would act as the stage necessary to make love.

I've made love to him many times but tonight when his dick entered my body; it felt better than it ever had before. His mouth covered mine again and his heavy breaths intertwined within my own. Hearing and feeling how much he wanted me, got my pussy wetter and wetter.

"Ummmm, this feels so good." I told him. "I love you so much."

"Damn, Kiante, your pussy stay tight. You don't let nobody touch my shit do you?"

"No, baby. This is all yours."

"I know this my fuckin' pussy. Shit! Damn!"

The dirtier he talked the closer my orgasm was coming. And I could tell by his short jerky moves that he was feeling the same.

"I'm 'bout to cum in that pussy, Kiante."

I didn't respond because I let go along time ago. Hempay knew how to handle me in the bed. Sometimes I'd pretend I was Lucia, and imagined how it was when he fucked her. And then I'd laugh to myself because now he was all mine. We stopped for twenty minutes after we came and when we got our second wind, it was time to go at it again. I decided to turn around and give him some of that back action. I didn't give it to him often, but when I did, he deserved it.

On my hands and knees I placed my upper body on the bed and raised my ass in the air. I could feel my cum dripping down my leg. I smiled when I heard him say, "Oh shit. You given daddy some of that sweet ass?"

There was no need to answer because he knew the deal. I just reached behind me and softly handled his dick and led him to my tight asshole. He rubbed the head of his hard dick back and forth on my presoaked pussy to get it lubricated. When he first entered me, every muscle in my body tensed up. But when I felt his warm strokes down the middle of my back, in addition to the way he sounded each time he went in and then out, I pushed back into him. For the first time ever when I fucked him this way, I felt myself cumming, too.

"I'm about to bust," he yelled grabbing my waist and pumping harder than usual. I knew I'd be sore later but I didn't stop him because it felt good.

"I'm cumming too, baby. Please don't stop!"

When he released inside of me, I felt his hot nut flood within me. Seconds later, I came too. He gently fell onto my body forcing me to the bed. As he lay on top of me, his breaths went from heavy to slower as seconds passed.

"You ready for the funeral?" he asked trying to catch his breath.

"After what you just put on me, baby, I'm ready for anything."

A Sad Day?

We all decided to pile into Hempay's Hummer. So everybody met us at the house and for a second, I shook my head at how the only reason we were together, was to go to Marissa's funeral. Raven, Karen, Mama, Daddy, Laila, Hempay and I all sat comfortably inside of his truck. As I looked to the left and beheld my husband's handsome face, my heart warmed as I was reminded that after all this time, we were still together. He gently placed his hand on my knee and winked, reminding me of the time we spent together last night.

"So how are you doing?" My father asked me from the back seat.

"I'm fine, daddy."

"I know my little girl's strong. I'm just sorry you have to do this. Marissa was such a nice girl."

"I know, daddy. But she really wasn't the same person you remember," I advised.

"Why do you say that?" My mother asked.

"Number one she kept obsessing over Lucia's face. She act like it was her fault. I couldn't stand being around her sometimes."

I could feel everyone looking at me suspiciously.

"Baby, you don't think that's a little rough?" My mother asked.

"Not really. I'm just telling you the truth," I told her as I went through my purse and reapplied my makeup.

"She's right, Mrs. Jenkins. Marissa and Lucia acted so different," Raven said as Karen co-signed by nodding her head.

Raven was only 5'4 but her voice was as loud and powerful as Lil Kim. She wore her hair in the same bun she had since we were in high school and freckles still shown throughout her bright yellow face.

"How would you know, Raven? Or you, Karen? Ya'll haven't seen the girl in years," Hempay interjected.

"And I didn't want to either. I saw Marissa in the mall a year ago and said hi and she walked away from me. What was up with that?" Karen questioned.

"I don't know," Hempay said as he merged onto the highway. "I wonder if it had something to do with the fact that both of you stopped being Lucia's friend when you got cool with my wife.

Makes me think it has something to do with her not looking the part anymore."

"Whateva, Hempay." Raven said. "Because if we're talking about Lucia, lets not forget who else betrayed her by getting with her sister's best friend!"

"Now, now kids," my father offered. "This is a tough time for everybody and there's no need in going at each other this way."

I heard my father but I wasn't sad. In fact I was happy the bitch was dead. I could no longer deal with her crying all the time and the guilty conscious she had developed. What made things worse was that she wanted me to feel guilty, too. But unlike Marissa, I had a life to live. What she want me to do, ruin everything I had going for me over Lucia? I don't think so.

When her face was first destroyed I spent as much time nursing Lucia back to health as she did. For months she never got out of bed. She'd piss and shit on herself and Mamma Maria, Marissa and I had to clean it up. After about six months later when she did get out of bed, she went only to the bathroom or she'd sit on the edge of the tub.

The entire time, she isolated herself from all of us. She only said our names when she was hungry, or wanted help putting the burn lotion the doctor gave her over her body. Outside of the three of us, she didn't want anybody seeing her face only to realize she wasn't the beautiful girl she use to be.

The only thing that remained was five holes that included her eyes, nose and mouth. She had no eyebrows, and no eyelids. The acid had completely demolished her facial features. We found out later that the damage was worse because her skin was supposed to be rinsed immediately. Instead, everyone panicked and wasn't smart enough to know what to do so she would pay for it the rest of her life. But despite her scars, from the waist down she was all Lucia.

For a while Lucia caused everybody to be sad but me. Out of everybody, no one took it harder than Marissa. I can't count the number of times she'd scream for Marissa to leave her room. And when she did, she'd remain at the door crying and begging to come back in. Lucia didn't say it but I knew Marissa's pretty face reminded her of how she used to look.

When I realized she didn't want to be seen, I took over the responsibility of running the Strawberry Cuties at school. I told them she wanted me to tell them certain things and they believed me since she never answered their calls and they knew I had contact with her daily. Before you knew it, they all accepted me. And from that point on life for me was perfect.

This brings me to how me and Hempay got together. For the longest time, he tried to be there for her. In fact, he tried for a whole year straight. He sent flowers, called everyday, tried to take her out and still, nothing worked. I told him to stop but he didn't listen. It was almost as if he felt responsible for what happened to her. I reminded him constantly that they weren't together before it happened and he should move on with his life, but at the time he didn't listen to me.

I knew I had to convince him that we were better together, and that no matter what, I cared about him. After awhile it worked. I can still remember the day I asked Lucia how she would feel about me and Hempay being together. When I walked into her room, I felt like I was getting ready to be judged. It didn't help that Hempay was waiting in their living room for the verdict. The stale smell of burn gels and Lucia not leaving the room for a year filled the air and added to the despair.

"You mind if I talk to you for a second?" I asked in a low voice as she remained sitting on the edge of her bed, looking toward the window. I knew that although her body faced it, she wasn't looking out of it. She was probably thinking about how her life was when she was a part of the world.

"Sit down," she responded her back still faced me.

I did as I was told and looked around her room. All of the mirrors were completely covered. She would've gotten rid of them if they weren't bolted to the dresser. So was anything else that could cast a reflection. Any remembrance of her past was gone including pictures. All that remained was a young woman who had been scarred for life.

"What do you want, Kiante?" Her back still faced toward my direction. Instead of asking her to turn around, I talked to it.

"Um...do you mind..."

Before I could finish my statement, she finished it for me. "No I don't. It was just a matter of time before he wanted to be with you anyway. Just so you know, I told him before he didn't need to waste his time on somebody who looked like me to begin with. It was Hempay who insisted on staying around."

"Don't say that, Lucia. He really cares about you and..."

"Please!" She responded abruptly cutting me off. "Do you think somebody who looks like Hempay, would actually want to be with this?" She asked as she turned around flashing me a glimpse of her face. I disagreed with her even though I knew she was right, not because her face was burned. Because as long as I lived, she'd never have Hempay, not as long as I wanted him. Besides, between how she looked and how she felt about herself, it would be difficult for anybody to love her let alone be with her. "Anyway you were gonna do what you wanted to anyway," she continued. "Why waste my time?"

"Listen," I started trying to get over how her face looked. No matter how hard I tried to get use to it, it never worked. "I know you love Hempay and I would never want to come between that. It's just that, I really care about him and I know he cares about me too. But we want to do this right. Not behind your back."

She started going into this psychotic hysterical laughter. Maria opened the door as if something remarkable happened that possibly erased all of the damage that was done to her daughter's face. When she realized things were all the same, she smiled at me and walked out the door.

"Don't you see, Kiante? You already have done it behind my back. The moment you showed him how you felt about him, before *any* of this happened, you were already between us."

"That's not true, Lucia! Me and Hempay were just cool."

"Yes it is true! Do you think I'm a fuckin' idiot just because my face is messed up?!"

Silence.

"I hope you and Hempay get everything you deserve."

"Come on, Lucia," I interrupted. "I care about you. We both do."

"Kiante, you don't care about me! You envied me."

"What the fuck I look like envying you?" I questioned.

"I guess your little nice girl routine went out the window huh?"

"It's not like that," I said remembering Hempay was out in the living room. I was prepared to give it to her but didn't want him overhearing us. "Listen, I may have looked up to you, but I never envied you, Lucia," I said as if I was trying to believe myself more than I was trying to prove it to her. "That's why I didn't understand why you would do that to me when we were in school."

"Looked up to me? Kiante, please! It has always been your plan to replace me. Now I guess it worked."

"Lucia, I'm sorry about what happened to you. But I didn't do it. You have to pick yourself up and stop feeling sorry for yourself."

"Kiante," she said as she walked over toward me. I could no longer hear what she was about to say because all I could do was focus on her face. "Take the life that you stole from me, and get the fuck out of my room! I don't want nothing else to do with you or him."

With that I picked up my dignity and walked out. Hempay who was sitting on the couch, turned to face me with hopeful eyes the moment he saw me appear.

"What she say?"

Silence.

"What she say, baby?" He repeated.

I was amazed at how important it was to him that she accepted us. What I really wanted to know was why? I couldn't help but think burns and all

154

that he still held a soft spot for her in his heart. Instead of telling him that she didn't want us together, I told him what she said first.

"She told me to she's happy for us and that she hopes we get everything we both deserve."

That started the beginning of our lives. It wasn't until our wedding day that he found out how much she really hated the idea of us being together after she rejected the wedding invitation he sent to her. Although a lot of people said we were wrong, most of them showed up, including Marissa even though she was drunk, Mamma Maria and J.D.

"How you holdin' up, baby girl?" Daddy asked again noticing me daydreaming still on the way to the funeral.

"I'm fine, daddy. This is just so terrible." I said attempting to sound sincere. "I understand, baby," he said. "She's in a better place. You did everything you could to help her. Everything!"

"If you need anything, sweetheart let me know," Mamma added. "I don't mind coming over and cooking for you and Hempay while you get yourself together."

"Don't worry about it, Ma," Hempay said in his soft compassionate tone. "Sarah's home and she's great. And if she needs anything else, I'm here for her."

"I keep forgetting ya'll have a maid," Mamma laughed. "I guess ya'll doin' pretty well for yourselves after all. I'm proud of you, Kiante. I'm proud of both of you." She said to me and Hempay.

This is why I loved my family. I finally have the perfect life. And it would've stayed that way if Marissa didn't up and kill herself. Why couldn't she do it somewhere she couldn't be found?! She is so selfish that she wanted people to feel sorry for her even in her death.

"I love that dress you're wearin', too!" Raven yelled from the back. "Where you cop that from? That's not the one we went shopping for." Her voice was loud and slightly inappropriate for the atmosphere of the day. No matter how much money Raven made, she will always be a ghetto girl from DC.

Hempay just shook his head because out of all of my friends, old and new, he hated Raven and Karen the most.

"I like it, too," Karen added. "I saw one just like it at Saks but it looked too plain for me." She added as if I purchased my dress from the Bargain Basement. "But you look cute in it though."

Karen stayed competing with me, but to hear her tell it, I competed against her. Lately it seemed like everything I bought, she had or was getting ready to buy. Hempay kept telling me stop competing with what he referred to as dizzy bitches but it wasn't about that. Sometimes I don't even know why I bothered telling him about some of the things that happened between me and my friends.

"Well I got my dress tailored because some of that stuff I buy from Saks even though it says size two, never really fits my waist. It'll probably fit you with no problem since you're a seven." I responded putting the ball back in her court. How dare that bitch try to play me in front of my husband.

"It's nice to see you girls are getting along considering the circumstances," my mother added sarcastically. That was her way of saying we shouldn't be worrying about clothes considering we were going to a funeral. Little did she know, the moment this was all over with, me and my girls had plans to go to the club tonight. It was a relief not having to worry if Marissa would get a change of heart and rat us both out about our involvement in burning Lucia's face. Telling our secret would not bring Lucia's face back.

"Mamma, we're trying to make the best of things, that's all." I advised. "It's bad enough we have to go to her funeral, we definitely don't want to think too much about it before we get there. It's sad enough as is."

"I know," she said breathing heavily. "The conversation just seems a little out of place that's all." She paused. "Anyway, did you bring Laila's raincoat? It looks like it's gonna rain." Mamma added looking at the sky.

Not that she wasn't right but the thing about that raincoat is this, I hated it. Her taste in clothes never changed and only got worse over the years. The raincoat was bright red with this thick multi colored insulation inside of it that Laila could barely walk around in. I'm so happy mamma's a psychologist at Children's Hospital Center in D.C. and wears those scrubs, because I shudder to think how people would react if she wore some of the giddy-ups in her closet.

"No, ma," I said taking a deep breath. "But Hempay brought her umbrella."

"I paid a lot of money for that raincoat, sweetheart," Mamma said disappointedly. "I wish you would let her wear it." Then she turned around to Laila. "Do you like the coat Grand Mommy bought for you, Laila?" she asked her.

"Yes," she said in her sweet voice. "It's my favorite. But mommy doesn't let me wear it at school when it rains."

Snitch!

"Well, make sure you wear it on the rainy days anyway okay? Your mother will let you," she said looking at me," she continued in the baby voice adults used when they talked to kids. To be honest, I don't know why we talk to kids like that. I'm sure they think we're idiots when we treat them like they can't understand any language outside of gibberish.

I went back and forth with my parents for a while as Hempay conducted business on the phone. Raven and Karen were keeping each other company while Laila listened to JoJo belt out ballads for the umpteenth time on her IPOD. All of our conversations ceased the moment we pulled up at the Stewart Funeral Home off of Benning Road in D.C. Hempay found two parking spaces to park in. Although his truck was not as large as a Hummer or Hummer 2, he didn't want anyone parking too close to him. Once we parked we hopped out. All of us slowly walked to the funeral, side by side. Almost all of the parking lots were full.

I immediately saw faces I recognized once we were inside. It was hot and more people were in attendance than I thought. Most of the people were from high school and I forgot about most of them the moment I got my diploma. Jamal was even there, and I was pleased when I saw he looked just like I left him, a hot mess. Right next to him stood dirty Chris even though he wasn't dirty anymore. Raheem on the other hand had been killed just six months earlier so he wasn't there. He was burned alive in his car after an accident. After Hempay spoke to a few people from Tyland Towers, he found out Raheem probably got killed after raping the sister of this dude who's doing time in D.C jail. He musta put the hit out on him from behind bars.

"Thank chu for coming," Mamma Maria said as she kissed me on the face and hugged Hempay, Raven, Karen, and my parents. "I'm having a hard time. But I tryin' real hard." She continued as the tears ran down her face. "It's jus that...it's jus that...I never thought I'd be burying one of my kids. Neva!"

While she was talking J.D, who was coming toward us bucked a U and walked hurriedly out of the funeral. Why? We paid it little attention though because Marissa was the purpose of today.

"How's Lucia?" My father asked like a concerned family member and friend.

"Not too well," Maria said shaking her head. "She not talk even more now." She continued wiping her tears with the handkerchief my father handed her.

"I'll pray for you and your family," My mother said as tears ran down into her face. Everybody was crying but I refused to. My mother was more emotional than I use to be and I don't think anything could make me cry anymore.

"Thank you," Maria said hugging my mother again. "I appre-che-ate that."

"What did the letter say?" I asked in a low voice. "The one you found in her room?"

"Kiante!" My father responded shocked at my question. I didn't mean to be rude; I just wanted to make sure she had actually taken our secret to the grave. Literally.

"It's okay, Mr. Jenkins," Maria smiled. "I couldn't read it, Kiante. I gave to Lucia. She has it now."

"Oh," I responded under my breath. "I see. Well," I said taking a deep breath. "I'll see you at the repast."

"Okay, sweetheart," she responded as she started crying again. "Lada."

Karen and Raven sat next to Chris and Jamal while Hempay walked with me to Marissa's casket. I had to admit, although I was happy this would all be over soon, I wasn't feeling looking at her body. Right before we reached the casket, we saw Lucia sitting in the front row wearing a black dress, a dark brown wig and a veil. After being burned, her hair, eyebrows and eyelashes could no longer grow so she looked even more peculiar. I was torn if whether or not I should speak to her, or leave matters alone. My dilemma was answered for me when Hempay reached out to Lucia first holding my hand.

"How are you doin'?" He asked softly placing his hand on her back. She jumped at first and than fell into it.

Hempay had a way of relaxing the most apprehensive of people. It was then that I realized that my husband was more physical with others than I liked. Why did he have to go around touching everybody as if he knew they wanted to be touched? Did he know? Whenever he laid hands on me before we were together, I never seemed to mind. I even remember the day in the kitchen when he hugged Mamma Maria right before promising to break J.D's jaw if he laid hands on her. I can still remember the look in her eyes as he held her in his arms. He had a way about him that did it for me and other woman. And that scared me.

"I'm fine, Hempay," her voice low and broken. "Thanks for askin'."

When she looked at me all I could do was stare. Her face. Her face was hideous. I didn't know what I expected, but I hoped it would change a little by now. I hadn't seen her in two years after I ended Marissa's and my friendship.

"Hi, Lucia," I let out. For some reason I felt uncomfortable talking to her. I guess I knew she didn't like me just as much as I didn't care for her.

"Kiante," she said looking at her bible. "You're doing well."

"Thanks," I said not knowing what that meant.

Before I could say anything else, Raven and Karen walked up. They hadn't seen Lucia but once since after the accident due to Lucia dropping out of school.

"You look pretty," Raven lied as she tapped Karen on the leg to cosign.

"Uh…yeah…you look real nice."

Please tell me why the fuck would they tell that girl that? I mean, do they think she's stupid? Her entire face is gone!

"Thanks," Lucia responded her eyes remaining on her bible. "But if you don't mind, I'd like to be alone now."

That was our cue to leave. Before I went to my seat, we all looked over Marissa's body. She didn't look anything like herself. Her face was dark and grey instead of creamy and light. Her hair looked brittle and not long and flowing like it used to be when we were in school together. After seeing Marissa and talking to Lucia, I had a feeling that the day would be longer than I realized. I was right.

REVENGE IS SWEET WHEN SERVED COLD

LUCIA

I sat in my room looking out of the window as usual. As if things couldn't get any worse, I lost my only sister and my mother wouldn't leave me alone.

"Chu hungry, baby?"

"No, ma. I told you that the last time you came in here."

"Lucia, you can't stay in your room forever. Chu have to come out and live your life. Marissa would have wanted it that way."

"What are you talkin' about, Mamma?! What life?! We buried my sister a month ago…people can't look at me five seconds without pointing fingers or questioning me about what happened and the love of my life has gone on without me! So please tell me, Mamma, what would you have me do?!" I yelled, my tears, unable to escape the tear ducts because they had been burned away.

"Live! I want chu to live, Lucia! Pleeeze! You have to at least try."

"Mamma, please stop putting me through the same shit over and over again."

"Watch how you talk to me, young lady! I am still you mother."

"Then stop pretending that things will change with me. You already know how I feel. Now please, get out of my room!" I was in no mood to hear her mouth.

"I love you, Lucia," she cried. "You still have people who love you, including J.D."

"Yeah okay, ma," I laughed as I turned around to look at my window and not out of it. "I'm quite aware at how much *J.D* loves me." I said, considering how much he fucks me every time he comes into my room behind her back.

With that my mother closed my door. Crying about my life was somethin' I wasn't gonna do anymore. I decided the moment I buried my sister that I'd bury any pity I had for myself right along with her. From here on out, my plan was to make the people pay, who stole my life away from me.

Kiante's funny. She had the nerve to prance into to church with her 3-carat ring with my ex-boyfriend, and friends, and speak to me. How fuckin' cold can you be?! I know they were laughing at me. It didn't make me feel any better seeing the little girl they made together. Luckily for me I have patience. Patience to do everything with time and the right way. Little do they know, my plan to destroy their lives includes her.

"Lucia," my mother interrupted waking me out of my sweet thoughts of revenge. "Jamal is here."

"Thanks, ma," I said as I put the wig back on my head and rearranged it to cover the fact that I didn't have eyebrows. "Send him back here."

"Lucia," Mamma said as if she was preparing to lecture me. "The living room is so much nicer. Why don't you come out here?"

"Mamma! This room is the only place I can go, where I'm in control of what people see and do to me. Now send him back here. I ain't got shit to do with you being embarrassed."

"One day you're going to miss me, Lucia. I swear it."

What she said went right in one ear and out the other. When Jamal walked into my room I could tell he was already high. I always wondered how new crackheads were formed since they knew what it did to you. You'd think they'd be afraid to look like zombies walking up and down the street. And since we still lived in the projects, Jamal had a chance to see them up close and personal.

"What up, Luc!" He said walking in and sitting on my bed. I hated when people sat on my bed with their street clothes on, especially now since my face is extremely sensitive due to losing so much skin.

"What took you so long to get the information?"

"I couldn't find that nigga! You know he got to keep moving because he got several hits on his head" he responded as he looked around my room for something to steal. "I thought I told you."

"You didn't tell me that. What you told me was that you knew where he was and that he'd be able to help me."

"I got you, boo!" he yelled as his eyes continued to search around my room.

"And don't bother checking shit out around here, Jamal, cause I ain't got nothin' in here you want, so you might as well stop lookin'."

"Well what *do* you got for me?" He shot back standing up.

"I got what I said I was giving you. Fifty bucks."

"Well what if I tell you the price has gone up?" Jamal responded trying to be greedy. "I mean, not everybody has access to him. I just happen to know him through my boy, but normally he doesn't talk to anybody else. He's doing me a favor."

He was so ridiculous that I started laughing. I could tell he was shocked by my reaction because he looked around like there was something behind him instead of his self that was hysterical to me. But my reasoning for laughing when people said stupid shit was simple. When you laughed in their face, it forced them to think about what they said without you having to repeat it.

Even though I laughed, I knew if he continued to fuck with me, he'd have more to worry about than just my laughing. I had enough money saved up courtesy of Mr. Hempay Carey to have Jamal killed if I wanted to. Right after my face was disfigured, Hempay started putting money into the account we shared together before we broke up. I told him over and over again that I didn't want it, but he continued to put no less than two thousand dollars in it a month. But when he got married it went from two thousand to one. You see Hempay was a thug but he had heart. He cared too much about the people he loved. And that was one weakness I had plans to use against him.

"What's so funny, you burnt faced, bitch?!" Jamal snapped at me. He was angry and decided to take it out on my face.

"You think you're hurting me by telling me something I already know? Well you ain't! But don't fuck wit' me, Jamal. There ain't but one thing I want in life and that's revenge. And if anybody stands in between that, I don't have a problem with reversing shit around."

Silence.

He sat down in the seat next to the mirror that most people took when they were afraid to face me and said, "His name is Ethan Stone. Well, that's the name he be tellin' mothafuckas and shit. But anyway, he can set up everything that you need. I ain't gonna lie, he's expensive. But if you really want it done, he's your man."

"I'm not worried about how much he's charging..."

"Then how come you only payin' me fifty bucks then?!"

"Cuz that's what you asked for," I reminded him. "But if you do right, there are other things you can do for me that I'll make sure you get paid for."

"Like what?"

"In time you'll find out. I just hope you have the heart to do it."

"As long as you're paying me I have the heart," he said reaching into his pocket. "Now here's his number. You can also reach him on this website he runs called dirtydicks.com. There are pictures of the people he uses on there. The faces are blanked out but their bodies are clear."

"You can't be serious!"

"I am serious. He said to tell you when you call to leave him a message. He never answers the phone because people are tryin' to sue him for all the shit he's done. Once you leave a message, he'll call you back within 10 minutes. If you don't answer the phone, he'll think it's a set up and won't call you back," he paused. "So you betta answer it. Who you gonna do this to anyway?"

"Why, Jamal?"

"I'm just akin'," he said as I handed him the fifty for the information. "You know who burned your face or somethin?"

"I got an idea. But you don't need to know more than I tell you."

"Well whatever you're doing, count me in," he said looking into my eyes.

Although Jamal was a mess, he never minded looking at my face. He didn't stare too long, or ask me too many questions about how it felt or how it happened, like most people did when they saw me. I guess being strung out on crack makes you worry about yourself and not others. I never thought I'd appreciate selfishness before I met him.

With Ethan's number in my hands, for the first time in a long time, I was happy that my plan was finally coming together. My mission? To destroy the Carey Family and ruin their lives for good.

It Happened Again
Kiante

I was sitting in the living room reading a magazine when my daughter rushed inside of the house.

"Mommy, mommy! It happened again," Laila yelled as she shot through the front door. "It hurt so bad."

When I heard the words leaving her mouth, the first thing I thought about was Hempay's threat. He promised to put a bullet into everybody at school if Laila got hit again.

"Come here, baby," I said trying to calm her down before Hempay found out. He was in the other room talking to his boys about the new shop they were opening in Eastover Shopping center in Maryland. "Listen, don't tell your father what happened," I continued removing her book bag and walking her over to the couch by her hand. "You understand?"

"No. Daddy said if it happened again to tell him."

"What's going on, Kiante?" Hempay asked appearing in the living room. "Why she cryin'?"

Shit! It was too late.

"I said what the fuck is goin' on, Kiante?"

"It happened again," I said under my breath.

"I know you didn't tell me somebody smacked my daughter again, did you? I know you just didn't tell me that, Kiante," he asked while walking over to Laila.

"Hempay, calm down."

"Calm down?" He questioned dropping base in his voice. "Somebody keep smacking my daughter and don't know body know shit when I go up there and ask who and why. You think that's nothin'? You too lax when it comes to her." He said inspecting every inch of her body.

"Hold up," I yelled placing my hands on my hips. "What the fuck you sayin'? I don't care about my daughter or somethin'?"

"What I tell you about cussin' in front of her, Kiante?" He said as if I was a child.

"Laila, go into the room," I told her. "I'll call you when we want you," I said handing her the book bag. Do your homework, too."

"Don't worry about your homework, Laila," Hempay said over talking me. "Just play with your toys. I'll be in there in a second."

When she was gone I was all prepared to get it on with him. He acted like he loved her more than me sometimes. I had her to show him how much I cared for him, not to replace me on a regular basis, but he always seemed so disconnected. This was one of the reasons I fucked around on him.

"What are you gettin' ready to do?" I asked Hempay as I saw him leave me and go toward the basement. I thought we were getting ready to talk.

"You know what I'm gettin' ready to do," he responded jogging down the basement steps with me close on his trail. "I'm goin' up to that school to blast their fuckin' heads open. It don't make no sense that they can't watch my daughter."

"Hempay," I said taking a deep breath. "Can you calm down please? If you go up there and do somethin' stupid, what you think gonna happen to Laila then? Where is she gonna end up without a father?"

"She's gonna be 'aight because I don't plan to get caught," he said opening up the lock box he had under the wooden paneling in the floor. "Click Click! I plan to get in and get the fuck out."

"Well what about me?" I questioned. "I need you." He examined the gun and closed the lock box and the panel on the floor.

"Look," he said looking into my eyes after tucking the gun into the back of his pants. "You gonna be 'aight. Both of ya'll. But what kind of man would I be if I keep allowing this bullshit to happen? That's my daughter man! And this is the third time somebody's slapped her in the face and ain't nobody seen shit."

"Hempay," I said breathing heavily. "It was probably one of her little friends. You know how

Laila can be sometimes. She's spoiled. So let's talk to her first."

"What the fuck are you talkin' about? Just cuz we spoil her means somebody gets to hit her in the face?"

"That's not what I'm saying."

"Well what are you saying?"

I knew coming at Hempay any other way but humble would make matters worse. But if I was going to get him to listen to me, I had to go another route and for some reason, the perfect idea entered my mind.

"Hempay, I'm pregnant."

"What?" He asked as his eyes lit up.

"I said I'm pregnant. Again."

"Are you serious?" he asked rubbing my shoulders.

"Yes, baby," I smiled and lied at the same time.

"Well why didn't you tell me?"

"Because I didn't know how you'd take it."

"Come here," he said walking me over to the leather couch. "If you woulda told me, I wouldn'tve gotten you all worked up."

"I wanted to be sure, baby," I smiled loving the attention he was giving. "I went to the doctor's today and it was confirmed. I'm having your baby. Again."

His look went from rage to concern and empathy. I had won him over with a few lies. I knew there would be no way he'd walk out that door and leave me in the condition I was in now. Next to Laila, nobody could reach him more than a new baby. He would be foolish to go to that school and pull his gun out on someone with me in my condition.

"Listen," he said with his hand on my flat and barren belly. "I'm not going up to the school, but we have to pull Laila out of there. I don't know how much more I can take of this shit. Because the next time it happens, pregnant or not, I have to handle my business. You understand?"

"I do."

"Aight. Now we have to take care of you." He hugged me. "Wow, you're really having my baby! I can't believe it!"

Whatever Hempay wanted was fine. I had worked so hard getting him that I didn't want to lose him, even if it meant that he couldn't defend our daughter's honor.

ONCE A SNEAK
ALWAYS A SNEAK
KIANTE

K aren and Raven were sitting at the kitchen table playing with Laila. Kiante said she was on her way and that it was okay for them to wait for her there.

"Why are ya'll still here if Kiante ain't?" Hempay asked as he prepared dinner for his wife and daughter. "Why don't ya'll come back later? Instead of asking me a million questions.

"We can't stay in here with you, Hempay?" Raven asked playing with Laila's soft hair as they sat at the kitchen table. "It's not like we don't go way back. We're basically family now."

"Yeah, Hempay," Karen added. "Ever since you got married to Kiante, you've been acting different. Like you don't know us and shit."

Hempay thought carefully about what he was going to say to their responses. Raven and Karen had a way with twisting his words around. It was a lesson he learned a long time ago when dealing with them. He also hated how they constantly threw monkey wrenches in his marriage, causing problems between him and his wife.

"I'm not acting different," he responded as he stole a sip of his beer, while mashing the ground beef with his fingers. "But I don't like the games ya'll be playin' either. Ya'll as scandalous as ya'll were in high school. You know why I don't fuck wit' ya'll like that. Ya'll were the main reasons me and Lucia didn't work."

"Aww....," Raven crooned. "You still miss Lucia."

"You know what I mean," he responded shooting her a stare. "Every time both of you come around, there's trouble."

"Well, Hempay," Raven said as she tapped Laila on her shoulder to get out of her lap. When she was gone, she walked over toward him, flung her long honey hair in his face. It brushed the ground beef. "Stop holding grudges. Like I said, we are family now, so there's no need in fighting us anymore. Besides, if we get along, so will you and Kiante. You know how it bothers her that you don't like us. You should try to be a little friendlier."

"Can you get your fucking hair out of my food?!"

"Sorry, I just want to get up close and personal with you."

As Raven stayed on his left, Karen moved to his right. "Yeah, Hempay," she cosigned. "Do you know how much fun we can have together if you play nice? There'd never be a dull moment we promise you. And best of all, it can be our little secret."

"What the fuck ya'll talkin' about now?" Hempay asked wishing he hadn't cursed since Laila was still in the kitchen, eyes glued on the scene and onto her father's face. "Hold up," he said cutting them off. "Baby, why don't you go watch the *Dora the Explorer* DVD, in the living room."

"I don't want to, daddy," she rebuffed. "I wanna stay here with you."

Hempay knew better. Laila was growing and was already inquisitive and she observed everything that was going on around her. At four years old, she could recite the names, dates and details of more information than Hempay or Kiante wanted.

"Baby," he said threatening her with his eyes. "What did daddy say?"

"Go watch Dora."

"And what does that mean?"

"I'm goin, I'm goin," she said plopping down from the chair at the kitchen table dragging her Dora stuffed animal with her. "Can you call me when you're finished with Aunty Raven and Aunty Karen? I want to play with them again."

Hempay didn't respond but it made him uncomfortable that she was so perceptive and attached to both of them.

"That was smart," Raven said moving in closer. "We wouldn't want Laila to see what we got planned for her father now would we?" She was shorter than Karen so her titties pressed firmly against his waist while her head rested on his muscular arm. "When you gonna let us remind you of how good we can make you feel? I know you miss it. Kiante can't be lettin' you hit it the way we did."

Hempay was trying his hardest to resist Raven and Karen but it was difficult, even though he couldn't stand them most of the time. To be the shortest out the two, Raven had the sex appeal and confidence to pull the most faithful of husbands down to their knees.

"I'm not fuckin' wit' ya'll," he said walking toward the sink to wash his hands although his dick was rock hard. "I'm married and it's as simple as that. So you might as well get out of here with that bull shit." As the water ran over his hands, he focused on his wedding band to give him more energy.

"Hem-pay," Karen whispered as she followed him to the sink. "Stop playing games," she continued grabbing his thickness in her hands. "You *are* gonna give us some of this, the only question is, when?"

When Karen licked her lips and blew a minty kiss in his face, Hempay grew two inches larger in her hands. He'd always thought they were sexy even in high school. And the three of them sexed each other up many of days on the funky mats inside of the gym after school hours. But now that he was married, and in love with his wife, he was trying to resist the urge. But instead of getting worse over the years, the two of them got sexier with time.

"I'ma be straight wit' you," he said looking at both of them. "both of you. What we use to do was tight, but I'm in love with Kiante. The only reason I ain't tell her how foul ya'll are is because at one point and time, I had my dick in both of your mouths. And I don't want no drama in my mothafuckin' house! But make no mistake," he said stepping away from the kitchen wearing a wife beater, Diesel jeans with a Gucci belt, "there ain't shit that can come between me and my wife. And if somebody tries to come between us, they won't be breathing."

"So it's like that now?" Raven asked.

"Exactly, like that."

Raven and Karen were furious that he rejected them again for the 10th time. Just like they had gotten more attractive, Hempay did too. His soft hair was pulled back into a pony-tail the way his wife liked it, and his beard was shaped up neatly on his face. They thought for hours on how it would be to fuck him while one was riding him as he ate the other's pussy.

"Well, forget you then, Hempay." They said sitting back down.

Thirty minutes later Kiante came home and the smell of meatloaf teased her nose. She found

Karen and Raven sitting in the kitchen tight-faced thumbing through a magazine. Hempay and Laila were in the living room watching Dora and immediately Kiante could sense the tension in the air.

"Is everything cool?" she asked them. "Everybody looks mad."

"Yeah. Things are real good." Raven responded.

"We were just bored out of our minds." Karen responded looking at Hempay.

When she said that, the moment Laila turned her head, Hempay threw the *Fuck you* sign up in the air.

TALL BLACK CUP OF COFFEE

KIANTE

"**M**rs. Carey, Raven and Karen are here," Jan one of my assistant managers said as I sat in my office at Starbucks. "You want me to tell your friends to come back here?"

"No, that's okay, Jan," I responded turning my computer off. "I'm coming out now."

When Jan left my office I jumped on the phone to confirm the dinner plans I had with my husband later on tonight. Ever since my friends were in my house the night I came home late, he'd been sexin' me up consistently. Almost as if he felt guilty about something. I was grateful for the attention, especially after he added more responsibility to my plate. Like the fact that Laila's new school, which he chose, was an hour away from the house and I was in charge of dropping her off and picking her up. I just wished he liked my friends more. It bothered me that he despised them so much.

Don't get me wrong, my life was already perfect, but if my husband would like my friends, I couldn't help but think that things would be a little better. I hated lying to him sometimes when I wanted to hang out just because I didn't want to hear his mouth.

"What is it about Raven and Karen that you don't like?" I asked him while we were working in the garden in our backyard one day. My garden is the bomb! I was growing herbs, spices and tomatoes. Our neighbors stayed coming over asking me what my secret was.

He looked at me as if he wanted to eat me alive because the shorts I was wearing had been fucking with him the moment I came out with them on. They gripped my pussy and every time I bent down, he could tell I wasn't wearing any panties.

"Baby," he said wiping the sweat off of his brow, smearing a little dirt on his face. "Why is it so important that I like them bitches? Most wives don't want their husbands hanging around their friends, and here you are pressin' me about it everyday!" He turned over the soil while the sun baked his beautiful skin, causing him to shine.

"Come on, baby," I started as I gave him a sip of my wine. "All my life I wanted to fit in and I feel I finally do. The only thing messing things up is that you don't like my friends."

"Kiante," he started as if he wanted to yell but thought better of it. "Them your friends, not mine! I'm never gonna like them bitches more than anybody I pass in the streets. So just leave it at that."

"But what is the problem? There has to be a reason, Hempay."

"Kiante," he said wiping the sweat off of his head again throwing down the hoe. "I'm not gonna like everybody you bring around me. All that matters," he said as he moved toward me, grabbed my ass and kissed my lips. "Is that we're together. I know you had some problems fittin' in when you were comin' up, but stop basing everything around what other people think. That shit is gonna cause problems for you one day if it ain't already happen." After that he let me go and said, "So don't ask me 'bout them bitches no more."

"Okay." I said under my breath.

"Oh…and why are you drinking wine? You're pregnant remember?"

I had forgotten about my lie. "You're right. You keep the rest."

"You gotta be careful, baby; you're carrying my baby now." He paused. "Again." He sipped all of the wine in my glass. "And drop the friend thing; I'm done talking about them bitches."

From that point on, I never asked him again. I just played my little tricks like inviting them over for dinner, hoping that sooner or later he'd change his mind about them. In a lot of ways he did come around because at one point, he didn't even allow them in the house.

I walked out of my office at Starbucks to greet my friends in the restaurant portion of my business.

"So where is he?" Raven asked before I could even sit down. "Because I hope you not trying to hook me up with no bum."

"Calm down, freak," I laughed joining them at the table.

"I know it's not the one over there with that bad ass suit on." We both looked in the direction she was looking in. "He's been staring over here for a minute." Karen said crossing her legs and blowing a kiss at him. "Cuz if that *is* him, I'm gonna be mad you hooked Raven up with him instead of me."

"Uugghhh!" Raven said hitting her arm. "That's some raggedy shit you just said. Anyway," she said smacking her teeth. "Have you forgotten about somebody?"

"Who?" Karen asked.

"Your husband, bitch. You're the one still attached not me. And until me and my man do get back together, I'ma have me as much fun as I can without him. So that's why she's hooking him up with me."

"Both of ya'll some nasty ass, freaks," I giggled. "But keep your voice down. I don't want my employees to know how nasty my friends really are."

"You can act all goody two-shoes for your employees but we know betta!" Raven advised. "And for your information, getting your pussy ate by somebody other than your husband is cheating too and it makes you just as nasty as us."

"Whatever," I said hoping none of my employees overheard.

"Now are you gonna keep talkin' my head off or are you gonna introduce us," Raven asked puckering her lips. "My biological clock is ticking."

Raven was terrible but I understood why she needed somebody to keep her company. Kink, her husband walked out on her at least once a year. And it was that time of the year again. We all knew that he only did it when he wanted to get back with his ex girlfriend Delamoni who was so pressed to be with him that she settled for the once a year break up that he gave her. The only reason Kink's unemployed ass didn't leave Raven permanently was because her fuck game was on point, and her money was even nicer. And after she showed me and Karen how she could suck the skin off of a banana with her arms tied behind her back, we believed her when she said she had him pussy whipped.

The guy I was introducing Raven to had been coming to my shop faithfully for the past month. At first I thought he wanted me, because whenever I came in with Karen and Raven, he was always looking in my direction. Later he built up the nerve to approach me, and asked me was Raven a friend of mine, and if she's available. Since at the time she wasn't available, I put him off until later. Now the time had come to bring them both together. So I called him over to our table.

"Martin Brooke, this is Raven Candela," I said as he shook her hand gazing into her eyes.

"Martin, huh?" She responded licking her lips. "I like that. I like that a lot."

"I'm feeling the name Raven too," he winked taking a seat next to me while Karen and Raven sat across from us. "And I'm feeling it a lot."

To say Martin was fine was an understatement, the only thing finer than him belonged to me and his name was Hempay. Martin's coal black wavy hair and his honey brown skin were on point. Just like Hempay, I could tell he got his beard cut by a razor instead of clippers because his edges were sharp. He was dressed in his smoke grey suit with fine pinstripes and smoke grey tie. He looked rich and he was just her type.

"What do you want with me, Mr. Brooke," she cooed already letting him know how horny she was by popping her lips as she pronounced each syllable in his name.

"I don't know, Miss Candela," he winked. "But I have a few ideas in mind."

"It's Mrs. Candela," she corrected him. "I trust that won't be a problem."

"Naw," he said shaking his head and licking his lips. "Whatever we do, will be between us. I won't tell him if you won't."

As the two of them conducted the War of the Wits, Karen and I marveled at how handsome he was. He was so fine that if I wasn't in love with Hempay, I would've never passed him on to Raven. He would've been the little toy I played with on the side from time to time.

"So what do you do for a living, Mr. Brooke?" Karen asked feeling left out.

"I'm a plastic surgeon specializing in burn victims," he informed us as one of the waitresses brought our coffee over to the table.

"Really," Karen asked with her hand under her chin as she nodded her head in approval. "A surgeon huh?"

"Yes, sweetheart," he responded flashing a sexual flirtatious smile that worked wonders for him. "I'm a surgeon."

"We have a friend who was burned by acid a few years back. Maybe if she had seen you, she'd look better than she does now. Because for real, she looks a hot mess." Raven advised sipping her coffee. "It's really sad because before that happened, she was a pretty girl."

"Really? That's awful. What happened?" He inquired as he leaned back into the chair.

"Nobody really knows," Karen interjected. "We startin' to think she may have done that shit to herself."

"What are you talking about, Karen?" I asked as I couldn't believe my ears.

"I'm serious. She was starving for attention from Hempay so who knows what she may have done."

"I see," he said as if he was concerned. "I would love to take a look at her if you don't think she'll mind. I mean, if you think it would help."

"I don't know about that," Raven said quickly.

"I would really like to try. Most of the work we do relates to patients whose conditions have worsened because of incompetent doctors. You'd be surprised at the significant changes we've made with a little time. Some of these doctors aren't fit to change a child's diaper let alone reconstruct someone's face but they still do it anyway."

"Well I don't talk to her no more," Raven interrupted. Even if he would've said he could cure her, Raven still would have held on to the information. Something in me decided that although Lucia hated my guts, it was my responsibility to get the message to her. Or maybe it was just that I wanted and needed a reason to keep in contact with him and this could be it.

"You really would be interested in seeing her?" I blurted out.

"Sure," he smiled. "You think she'd be open to my help?"

"I'm sure she would," I smiled, feeling the stares from Karen and Raven. "She's been living in her room for over six years because she's too embarrassed to come outside."

"Why you getting involved, Kiante?" Karen asked as she combed her hair with her fingers. Her hair was as healthy as Marissa and Lucia's use to be. I smiled when noticing a strand of her hair had fallen down into her coffee. I wasn't about to tell her either. "You know she don't want you in her bizness, especially since you married Hempay. You should leave things alone."

Was she putting my business on front street in front of Martin? Because it sure seemed like it. Instead of getting stupid I said, "Well I would *think* that if you had some information that would change my life, you'd tell me. I'm just doing the same thing for Lucia."

When she fought to get the hair out of her mouth, she sipped from her coffee and I laughed to myself. Bitch!

"Do what you want," she continued. "But don't say nothing to me when she goes off on you. You were warned."

"Well let me give you my card," he said smiling at me. I felt the texture of the card and it was a little flimsy for a man in his line of work. It felt as if he'd ran a few copies off at Kinkos. After realizing I was thinking too much on something that didn't matter, I took his card and slightly brushed my index finger over his thumb. He smiled and said, "Call me if you get in contact with her and you think she may want my help."

"What about me?" Raven responded blowing him a kiss. Usually Raven's flirt game was off the chain, but now it was borderline trashy. "Do I get a card, too?"

"Sure, sweetheart," he said winking at her. "Make sure you use it, too."

"Trust and believe," she responded. "I will."

As he handed her his card there was one thought that had entered my mind, I guess that makes two of us who had plans to call the good doctor.

If there's three things I love in life, it's being black, sexy and rich. And to think, I almost didn't make it out tonight but Raven and Karen begged me for two weeks straight. Lately I had been focusing on Hempay and getting Laila up and running in her new school that I forgot to have fun. Plus my parents had been over three times within the past few weeks staying a few nights at a time. Normally I only saw my parents once a month because my mother was on call, and Daddy's business had taken off. So although it was nice spending time with them, tonight was for me.

It was kinda cute to see us all sitting around laughing and talking about our lives. Three generations together and there was nothing but love. Laila would run around showing everybody how she could stand on her head while we all encouraged her. My father sat on the couch with Hempay discussing investment strategies. Now that they had the same accountant, they'd spend a few hours a week talking about how their portfolios were looking. Every now and again he'd mention how close he was getting to saving enough money to marry my mother in Jamaica again, something he never got to do years ago because he was taking care of me. His plan included airfare and hotel fare for everybody he invited. Yeah, my family life was in order, but for some reason, I always wanted more.

After kicking it with the family, it was time for Raven and Karen and I to leave out. I hadn't been out of the house for weeks and Hempay had gotten use to me being around. So when I told him I wanted to go out, he gave me shit. He was doing everything in his power to get me to cut them off and I never understood why. After a fight we had about Laila, I used it as my excuse to go out anyway. I put on my white linen dress that fit my body for the linen party at H20 in D.C.

Once we made it to the club I wasn't surprised to see attractive people everywhere dressed in all white. I was feeling the scene and I knew all I needed was a drink to set things off.

"I still ain't seen his fine ass," Raven complained as Busta Rhyme's *Touch It* pumped in the background. "I'm startin' to think he's gay or somethin."

"You always think somebody's gay," I laughed.

"I'm serious! Why else wouldn't he return my calls?" Raven paused. "If he doesn't want a taste of this pussy something has to be wrong with him."

"You may be right," I yelled feeling the euphoria that could only come from drinking three dirty martinis back to back. "I knew he was too good to be true."

"Right!" Karen added. "Ain't nobody that fine single."

"Exactly," Raven laughed giving her a high five. "But I wasn't tryin' to marry him. I was tryin' to fuck him! That bitch could've had him back after I got finished with him."

"So what's up with you and Kink anyway?" Karen asked sipping on her Belvedere straight up. "Ya'll ain't back together yet?"

"NO!" Raven responded spinning the red straw in her cup. "And I'm not thinking about him right now either. I'm tired of his ass leaving me three weeks out of every year to crawl back to that bitch. It ain't like I'm in his pockets or asking him to do this and that for me. I take care of his broke ass! I'm thinkin' about cuttin' him off for real."

"Where he staying at now?" I asked. "With her?"

"Who knows," Raven responded shrugging her shoulders. "He claims he's staying over Dinky's house. But every time I go over there, he claims Kink ain't there. Our marriage is all the way fucked up."

"Dinky?" I asked to be sure I heard her correctly. "I didn't know he still kept in contact with him."

"Yeah," she laughed. "You know they best friends or some shit like that. I think he has a lot to do with the problems we have right now. He's more into our personal business than we are. Sometimes Kink can't make a move without asking him about it first."

All I could think about was that the last time I heard about Dinky was when I was with Marissa when we were kids. Every now and again I'd think about how she shaved her pussy meaning it to read Dinky when it actually read Dicky. But what really stood out in my head was how both of us use to think he was gay. And the last thing I heard, he had come out of the closet.

"How long they been friends?" I asked as I tapped my white stiletto shoes to the beat of *What You Know* by T.I.

"All their lives," Karen responded for her.

"Humph," I paused. "That's a little strange."

"Strange?" Raven repeated. "Why you say that?"

"Ya'll never hear anything about Dinky being gay?" The liquor threw my tactfulness out the window. I felt it was important to get right to the point.

"I heard that shit before," Raven said. "But trust me; Kink ain't hardly thinking about being gay or fucking with a man when he got me. My pussy too good to make him think about going the other way. *Anyway*...he told me Dinky had a girl living with him."

"Dinky is not fucking with Shawanda. That bitch don't even wash her ass," Karen added.

"You sure they ain't just roommates?" I thought out loud.

"No they aren't just roommates!" Raven said smacking her tongue. "I like how you tryin' to say my husband is gay."

"I'm not saying that, Raven," I responded. "I'm just keeping it real with you because it doesn't sound right. Plus the fact that he keep rolling out for weeks every year is getting played. I wouldn't be going for that shit. Something is up with him."

"You act like all men are perfect," she said looking at Karen. "I'm sure Hempay has shit with him too that you don't know about."

"What are you trying to say?" I questioned looking at them both for answers.

"I'm sure Hempay has secrets you don't know anything about," she continued. "Just like I said. So keep that in mind when you think you're Mrs. Cosby."

"I'm sure he has secrets, but I do know this. Whatever they are, it doesn't involve another man." I advised as I pointed my French manicured index finger at her for emphasis. "That much I am sure about."

"Well you betta hold on to him," Karen laughed. "Because somebody might snatch his fine ass."

"No," I corrected her. "Somebody may try."

It was getting heated in the VIP section we occupied at the club. And because I started the tension by insinuating that her husband may be gay, I decided to break the ice by buying us all another round of drinks. After awhile, we were feeling so good, that we couldn't believe our eyes when Martin walked in.

"Is that who I think it is?!" Raven asked as she looked in his direction.

"It sure looks like him," Karen responded.

"Yes girl it is!" I said excitedly. I was so enthused about seeing him, that both of them cut their eyes at me. "He looks better now than he did when I first met him."

"Hold up," Karen said. "Is he for you or Raven?"

"Right, bitch," Raven added. "Why you getting so excited?"

"I'm married but I'm not blind. He's killin' that linen suit."

"We can see," Karen commented. She had a thing for being an instigator. She never really had her own opinion or her own mind. "But calm down. I don't want him thinking we're tripping off of him."

"Go talk to him for me, Kiante." Raven asked from nowhere. "I want to know what's up with his missing in action scene."

"What?! What will I say?"

"Ask him why he hasn't returned my calls." She responded hitting my leg. "I'm tired of playing phone tag. Shit if he says the right thing tonight, maybe I can see what he has hanging between his legs. I mean, I'm ready if he is!" she giggled.

"You're a gross bitch," Karen laughed. "But I'm not mad at you."

I thought it was funny how a few minutes earlier she was saying she's not tripping off of him. But now that he's here, she's had a change of heart.

"Why don't you do it yourself?" I asked her. "It seems real young if I do it for you."

"Because you hooked us up," Raven said as if I should've known. "And if I go over there it'll seem like all I've been doing is thinking about him."

"I think it will sound stupid if I do it," I advised. I know it was wrong but something in me did not want to talk to him about her. I wanted to know if he ever thought about me.

"Never mind, Kiante," she responded. "If you can't do this for a friend I guess you're not my friend to begin with. "Come on, Karen," she said grabbing her by the wrist. "Let's go get some drinks."

"Wait a minute!" I said looking at them both. "I'll do it."

"Thank you, girl," she said wrapping her arms around my neck as she hugged me. If she jumped one more time I'm sure her titties would've fallen out of the strapless dress she wore.

When I got up and walked toward him, for some reason I began to sweat. I was so nervous that perspiration ran down my legs. I hoped it wasn't visible the closer I got to him. From afar he was handsome but now that I was close I saw how truly attractive he was. Suddenly I was horny and wanted nothing more than to press my lips against his. I wasn't thinking about my family or losing the home we built together. I replayed the fight over and over again me and Hempay had in the house to get me pumped to do whatever I wanted to do. And I certainly wasn't thinking about putting in a good word for Raven either. This boy toy would be all mine.

"Martin," I said tapping him softly on the shoulder.

When he turned around his face lit up the moment he saw mine. "Mrs. Carey, how are you?"

"Better now." Where did that come from? Oh my Gawd I'm acting like a complete whore. "I mean, I'm fine."

"I know how you look but I want to know how you're doing," he smiled. For a minute he turned me off with that weak line but I let it go.

"I'm doing great, Martin," I giggled. "Just out enjoying myself."

As we looked each other over as if we were the only ones in the room, Jamie Foxx's *Unpredictable* song danced throughout the room. This was the wrong song to be playing right now because that's exactly how I felt about tonight.

"I came over here to talk to you about something," I responded in a fake attempt to put in a good word for Raven.

"If you came over here to talk about anything or anybody else but you, to be honest, I don't want to hear it," He said respectfully but with seriousness in his voice.

I didn't know what else to say. Even if I had planned on telling him that Raven was the woman for him and that he'd be a fool for not getting to know her, he made it clear that he wasn't interested.

"So," he continued clearing his throat. "What do you want to talk to me about?"

"I...umm....forgot."

"Walk with me," he said reaching out his hand.

When he led the way, I turned around and threw Raven the *Everything's Cool Symbol* as if any moment now he'd be getting down on one knee and proposing to her. When we finally reached our destination, we were sitting on the other side of the room in another VIP section, completely out of view from Raven and Karen. All of the women were turning their heads as we passed because Martin was just that fine.

"Why have you been on my mind?" He asked me as if I knew the answer. "Ever since I had an opportunity to meet you, you're all I think about."

"I don't know," I responded looking at my shoes. "You tell me."

"I wish I could tell you, Kiante. All I can say is, I had all intentions of getting to know your girl better, but after I talked to you, I'm feeling as if we could have something more. A better connection."

"But…"

"Before you say anything, I know you're married. And you should know that if nothing else materializes out of this relationship, I'm cool with your friendship."

"Relationship?" I asked trying to give off the impression that I was uninterested.

"You know what I mean," he winked. "I can see it in your eyes that you're feeling me."

"You're pretty high on yourself aren't you?"

"No…just confident."

"Well why are you so confident when it comes to me?"

"You tell me? Am I wrong or are you feeling me the same way I'm feeling you?"

"Who are you?" I asked. In my mind he was perfect, and a part of me -- the sober part -- felt guilty for wanting him. But the more I drank, the more the sober part was dying taking my conscious right along with it. "You seem a little unreal."

"I'm a man who hasn't met a woman who can keep my interest long enough to get me curious until now."

"You can get any woman you want."

"That's not it. I haven't always looked the way I do now. I grew up never really knowing my place. And with all the money I have now, and everybody around me, sometimes I still feel alone."

"Sometimes I feel the same way, too!" I exclaimed. "I was the outcast in school and although my life is on point right now, sometimes I feel as if things could be better or different. It's almost as if I'm missing something but I don't know what."

"I get that from you. I wonder why?"

"Sometimes I feel like I have...like I have...someone else's life."

"I see." He paused. "What about your friends? Are you cool with them?"

"Sometimes," I said in a low voice but loud enough for him to hear me. "I'm not sure if they're really down for me though. We met under some messed up circumstances."

"Yeah," he said as if he went somewhere else. "I had only one friend coming up in school. Don't get me wrong, I'm my own man, but when you live in the projects, it's hard to find your place if people really don't want you around. On top of all that, you have to keep checking the people you do allow in your circle."

I couldn't believe this fine ass man went through anything similar to what I went through. All I wanted to do was spend the rest of the night with him picking his mind. It was that reason alone that reminded me that I needed to leave. We were bonding on a level closer than sex and I couldn't have that in my life right now.

I was preparing to say my goodbyes when a woman approached us and jumped in his face. She was shaking and pointing at him like she couldn't believe he was there.

"You ruined my fucking life! You dirty bastard! You ruined my fucking life?!"

The tall woman was irate and causing a scene right in front of our area. Whoever she was, she wasn't happy about seeing him with me. "Ma'am, you must have me confused with someone else," Martin responded in a cool respectful tone. As stupid as she was acting he still remained calm. If I was him, I would have hauled off and slapped her in the face.

"I know exactly who you are and I'll hate you for the rest of my life!" Her light complexion was red with rage.

"Ma'am," I offered trying to calm her down. "He and I are just friends."

"I don't care who he's dealing with," she yelled causing a spit drop from her mouth to fall on my lip. "He'll just ruin their lives, too!"

"Sir," the security guard interjected. "Is everything okay here?"

"There seems to be some misunderstanding," Martin said. "Apparently I remind her of somebody she hates."

"Would you like me to escort her out?" The security guard asked.

I waited patiently to see what kind of person he was. Agreeing to throw her out to me would mean she was right about him, but to allow her to stay meant she probably did have the wrong person. She remained there waiting on his answer too as her friend tried to convince her softly to walk away.

"No," Martin responded looking at the security guard. "I don't mind if she stays just as long as she promises to stay out of my way. I'm just trying to enjoy the rest of the night with my lady."

My lady? Why did that sound so good to me?

"You're a good man," the guard said, extending his hand for Martin to shake before directing his attention to a still very mad woman. "Come with me ma'am." He said gripping her arm as she fought with him to get at Martin.

"There's something about you that pulls me," I started. "I don't know why, but it's true."

"What you feel is mutual."

I smiled. "Still, I'm a married woman who is in love with her husband. So I'm gonna have to go now. Sorry," I responded.

That was the last thing I remember saying before....

"Damn, Martin," I moaned with my hands on the back of the toilet in the woman's bathroom so he could get it right. "Hit this pussy."

"What you think I'm doing, girl?" he boasted pulling my hips to him over and over with quick rough strokes.

His dick felt almost as good as Hempay's. The only difference was that because I was his wife, he didn't believe in yelling obscenities at me. That's why sometimes the perfect stranger fucks were the best. I loved to have sex while cussing in between.

As he continued to hit it from the back, I was working on my second orgasm and he hadn't even gotten his first. I could tell it was all about pleasing me. People were coming in and out of the woman's bathroom but we didn't care. As cheap as it was to be having sex with a perfect stranger, I was mentally writing it down in my head as one of the best sexual experiences in my life. When he was about to cum he said, "Kiante."

"Yes, baby," I responded my voice low and lustful.

"I want you to do something for me."

"What is it, baby?" I asked my body being moved in short jerking motions.

"I want you to take me in your mouth. Can you do that for me?"

Maybe if I was sober I would've said no. Instead I thought about getting pregnant since we *were* having sex raw. I rather take his nut in my mouth and not worry about getting pregnant. Whenever the thought entered my mind about contracting HIV I pushed it out. Anyway he was a doctor and doctors don't have that kind of shit right? They have to be safe. They probably wouldn't even allow him to work around people if he was HIV positive. After forming my own conclusions, I decided to make this a night to remember for him too. I wanted him to be thinking about me as much as I'm sure I'd be thinking about him once I left. I had already crossed the line of being freaky so there was no turning back now anyway.

"Okay, baby," I said positioning my body to meet his request. "Let me taste that for you."

With me sitting on the edge of the toilet, he grabbed the back of my head and said, "Kiante...open wide."

"Yes, Martin." I smiled. "Anything you want."

I opened my mouth and he filled it with nut. Drunk and a little out of my mind, I swallowed every drop.

"I want you to call me something now that you've drank my babies."

"Sure, I smiled. "I'll call you anything you want." I responded looking up at him.

"Alright, baby," he said softly touching my cheek. "If you ever see me again, I want you to call me Blaze."

A Step Closer

LUCIA

I was sitting in my bedroom, happy about how the plans were coming together. Kiante had fallen for my bait and now it was time to take shit to the next level.

"He's not as easy as she was," Ethan said as I listened to him on the phone in my bedroom. "I sent the girl you picked out from the website, and another one after that and Hempay shot them both down. He seems to be faithful to his wife."

"I don't want to hear that shit," I said. "All men can be broken down." I paused. "Did they go to his barber shop?"

"Yep," Ethan laughed. "The other men in the shop hit on the girls you picked but Hempay didn't pay either of them any attention. Your boy's in love with his wife, Lucia. Now normally I don't turn down money. But if you keep trying to entice him with females when he's not interested, you're gonna come up broke. Maybe you should leave this one alone."

"Well what did their faces look like?" I asked because although I picked out the ones I thought were most likely to get Hempay's attention, their faces were blocked out to protect their privacy. But all the women on the site were said to be extremely attractive.

"They were Latino."

"I know that! But how did they look?"

As I waited for his answer, I thought it was puzzling to me that he ran a business from the internet to infect people with diseases. But for my purposes, I'm glad that he did.

"Everybody I have working for me is appealing. Trust me, both of them were beautiful," he advised. "He just wasn't interested. It happens sometimes. The man is in love with Kiante."

"It doesn't make any sense! If they were pretty, he would've been interested! I know him okay! You don't!" I yelled. I hated to think that Hempay didn't take the bait because he was actually in love with that bitch!

"Like I said, maybe he's faithful. My business is designed to get those who deserve it for cheating on their spouses. Not those who are innocent. And Hempay is one of the good guys."

"Yeah right," I laughed. "If he was so faithful, he never would've gotten with Kiante in the first place. I was his girlfriend, okay? He was with me!"

"Oh…so that's it. You're still upset about an old relationship you had with him. So tell me Ms. Lucia, what is your story?" He asked.

"What is yours?!" I redirected. "There aren't too many people who run a business based on giving people infections."

"Is that what you think I'm *all* about?" He asked as if he couldn't believe how I felt. "Giving people infections."

"Yes."

"Well that's not what I'm about. I don't run around hurting *innocent* people, just the ones who cheat. My wife gave me HIV after sleeping with my best friend who was positive. Ever since then, I vowed that people who stepped out on their spouses deserved to get what was coming to them. Now if I make a little money on the side, what difference does it make?"

"How do you even find these people?"

"They come to me from advertisements. They were fucked over the same way I was so I'm doing the world a public service."

"Please," I laughed. "You're just as guilty as the ones who cheat. Who do you think you're hurting when you give people incurable infections? Their wives, husbands, boyfriends and girlfriends. They get it too. In fact, if things work out, Hempay should be infected any day now anyway. So cut the self righteous bullshit!"

"Just make sure my wire goes through tomorrow!" He yelled feeling upset I pulled his card. "I want my fucking money."

"Didn't the last one go through?!"

"Yes."

"Well, so will the second. You just make sure your boy keeps this between us."

"Oh he will," he laughed.

"Later." I said.

"Wait. Before you go, why did you want him to call himself Blaze while he was having sex with your target?"

"Because I wanted her to sleep with one of her lies; and…I wanted her to know I had something to do with it when she realizes she has herpes."

"You're almost as cold as me," he said.

"Naw…," I laughed. "I'm the coldest person you'll ever know."

THE TRUTH HURTS AGAIN

KIANTE

"**Y**ou did what?!" Raven yelled in the dining room of my home. I invited Raven and Karen over to talk to them, because of what happened between me and Martin in the bathroom. I wasn't sure, but I had a strange feeling that Lucia had something to do with it. When he told me to call him Blaze, I knew my past had come back to haunt me.

"I had sex with him in the bathroom at the club," I responded with my head hung low. I focused on the soft voice of Keyshia Cole's *I Should Have Cheated* instead of the shame I felt inside. I had turned the stereo on to conceal my deceit from anybody who wasn't a part of the conversation.

"If you wanted him in the first place," Raven yelled. "Why did you introduce him to me?!"

"Is that all you think about?" I questioned.

"It's not all I think about, but what you did is pretty fucked up."

"Well it wasn't even like that, Raven," I cried shaking my head. "I was drunk and one thing led to another. He took advantage of me."

"Oh so what?" Karen interjected. "Now he raped you?"

"You might as well say that he did," I advised. "You know how much I love Hempay."

"It doesn't make any sense that you would leave us and go into another room, and then end up in the bathroom." Karen added. "And if he raped you, why didn't you call the police?"

"Because I didn't want Hempay to find out."

"Well I think you're lying," Karen responded.

"That's not fair," I said trying to explain my piece. "Don't act like you haven't done something before you weren't proud of."

"Yes I have, Kiante, but must you sleep with everybody's man?! No man is safe around you."

"He didn't belong to Raven, Karen!" I advised growing angry. "And what happened between me and Lucia was different than this."

"Is it?" Raven asked with her hands on her hips. "Cause to me, it looks like you're at it again. Hempay was with Lucia, you wanted him and you stole him from her; during one of the toughest periods in her life, too."

"Why are we letting a man come in between our friendship?" I asked looking at their eyes for buy-in. "Ya'll act like I fucked one of your husbands."

They both looked at each other and I felt I was reaching them so I continued, "I'm only telling ya'll this because things have gotten worse. Way worse. And I need my friends to be there for me."

"Don't tell me that you up and got pregnant, Kiante! Cause that's gross," Karen said.

"No, it's not that."

"Then what is it?" Raven asked while eating a piece of one of the sandwiches Sarah made for us.

"The past couple of days I've been getting these sores around my mouth."

"Uuuughhh!" Raven laughed. "Does that have something to do with Martin? Cause if it does, you did me a favor by stealing him."

"Yeah," Karen asked moving in closer to inspect them. "What is that shit on your face anyway?"

"Can ya'll stop acting dumb for five minutes!" I yelled. "I'm serious!" I wasn't feeling the third degree they were laying on me when I was trying to tell them what was going on. They were supposed to be my friends but here they were finger pointing and laughing at my predicament.

"Yuck…This shit on your lip is a mess," Karen added. "You didn't let him put his dick in your mouth did you?"

You know there was no way on *earf* I was telling her yes, especially after they gave me the blues already. It hurt me that they were talking to me as if they didn't know me. Because if either one of them would've come to me with the same scenario, I would've been supportive and understanding.

"You sure you don't have Herpes?" Raven asked before I could answer the question.

"I don't know what I have. I know it has something to do with that night though. But what I want to know is why do I get the feeling that both of you don't care?" I asked.

"We care, but at the same time, what you did was fucked up, Kiante! Dang!" Raven responded. "I woulda neva pegged you to do some raunchy ass shit like that." Her phone began to ring and she ignored it at first. But when it continued, and she couldn't get the rest of the hate off her chest, she decided to answer it. "Hold on for a minute, Kiante," She paused as she answered her cell phone and listened for a second at the caller. I could hear faint words before she said, "Tony, I don't care how much is costs, this is a major fucking account!"

"Is that Tony?" Karen asked as if she was waiting for his call too.

Raven nodded her head yes and stood up to walk toward the window. "Listen, this is not something we want to play with! It took us a while to get the MacArthy account, and if we half step on the roll out of their new hair care products, we'll lose it." She paused. "Uh huh," she continued as she shook her head and listened to him on the other line. "Uh Huh, yes. Uh huh. Okay. Uh huh."

As she continued on with a conversation, I wondered if I made a *major* mistake by revealing my infidelities to them. What had me vexed was that it wasn't like they never cheated on their husbands before. And Karen know she better stop playing because she got pregnant by the 16 year old boy who mowed her lawn while she was married. And who was it that took her ass to the clinic to get an abortion? Me! Not Raven but me. She didn't even feel comfortable telling her what happened because she knew I could keep secrets and Raven couldn't.

Slamming the phone closed she shook her head to Karen as if the conversation ended on a bad note. All I could think about was that I hoped whatever she heard, was bad enough to make both of them leave my house. Suddenly, I wanted to be alone.

"Look," Raven started as she took a deep breath. "I'm not trying to be mean, but what you did in the bathroom was some whore ass shit. It's just as simple as that. So if you thought we were gonna condone that bullshit, you got anotha thing coming. I'm not goin' to sugar coat anything for you. A true friend wouldn't do it."

"Exactly!" Karen said as if she was thinking the same thing but didn't have the nerve to say it. "You were dead wrong and now you have to pay for it. The most I can say is go to Doctor Leonard's and see if he can give you something for it."

"I know that it was messed up," I said wishing I hadn't told them bitches shit. "But it happened now and I'm asking for ya'lls help."

Was she that mad about not getting Martin or whatever his name was that she was unwilling to help me? I began to wonder if they were the same way to Lucia when they were friends. In high school they told everybody they were sisters and the closest friends ever. And now that I think about it, both of them often tell people they are my sisters too. It would be fucked up to discover that the awesome life I thought Lucia had, really wasn't so awesome.

"Forget I ever told ya'll. I have to think of things on my own right now," I said dismissively.

"Well it's not that easy," Raven said. "Now we do know."

As she was talking for some reason, I thought about the woman who was in the club and how she said he ruined her life. Everything was finally making sense to me; he probably gave her the same thing he passed on to me.

"What about Hempay?" Raven asked still standing up with her hands on her hips. "How you know you ain't give it to him? Cuz I'm sure you had sex with him since Martin gave this shit to you."

"Hold up," I said as my nose stung letting me know I was getting ready to cry again. "Why are you asking me questions about my husband? He's my responsibility not yours."

"I know he's yours. And I'm your friend," Raven responded. "But you need to know only hoes get down like that. What if you gave it to Hempay? Then what you gonna do?"

"Right cuz if you got Herpes you're stuck. Cuz ain't no cure for that shit! Once you got it that's it."

"I don't know what I'm going to do," I said raising my hands in the air. "I don't know. That's why I called both of you!"

After feeling a headache coming on, I asked Sarah to bring me some Hennessy to pour in the coffee I had been nursing. Friends are supposed to make you feel better not worse.

When I heard Hempay come through the door with Laila with him, my heart sank. The mood was so thick now that I could barely move. And because Hempay was always in tune with things going on around him, I knew he'd know something was up.

"Mommy! Mommy!" Laila said as she ran up to me. I almost gave her a kiss until I realized what I had on my mouth. If I would have given my baby herpes, I would've jumped out of my window from the third floor.

"Hey, baby," I said squeezing her and giving her a hug instead. "How was your day?"

"Goood! But why don't you wanna kiss, Laila?" she asked bringing attention to what was dreadfully apparent amongst me, Raven and Karen. "Laila wants to kiss mommy."

"Cuz I may be sick and I don't want you to get it," I lied looking at my so-called friends for support. "How was your day?"

"It was fun! We saw Chucky Cheese and we got to play the piano and everybodee was dancing and we fell down," she rambled on for 40 seconds as all of her childhood thoughts began to come together.

"That's good, baby," I said smiling as I felt the eyes of Raven and Karen's judgmentally watching me.

"Hey, baby," Hempay said as he reached in for a kiss. "I'm a big boy. I'm not worrying about getting sick. Give me some of that suga."

I gingerly smiled and puckered up my lips real big so that he would kiss me on the fleshy part that didn't have the sore.

"That thing's getting bigger ain't it," he inquired. "Did you see the doctor yet?"

Before I could respond Karen said, "I think you should tell him, Kiante. It's only right that he knows."

"Tell him what?!" I said as I shot a look at her that almost knocked her to the floor. Was this actually getting ready to happen? I know this bitch ain't getting ready to out me in front of my husband. My heart felt like it was getting ready to pump out of my chest. "Go upstairs, baby," I said praying he'd listen to me. "Let me finish up with Karen and Raven."

"Naw," he said shaking his head. "What are you talking about?" He continued looking at her for answers. "It's obvious you think she should let me know something. So you tell me what it is."

"Your wife was fucking somebody in the bathroom at H20, and apparently she got a case of the Herpes," Raven advised caring nothing for me, my marriage or my feelings.

I fell out of the seat and Hempay on reflex picked me up. When I was upright. He looked down at me and than back at them trying to take in everything that she said. I couldn't offer him any consolation because what she said was true. If I lied, and it turned out I was infected, he would've remembered this day and thought everything I ever said before then was a lie. This turned out to unexpectedly be the worse day of my life. I could never have seen this coming. Both of them were supposed to be my friends when in actuality, they were my enemies. All I could think about was that if he stayed with me after this, I'd focus on my family leaving all outsiders out, starting with the two of them.

"What's going on, Kiante?" he asked now holding Laila in his arms. "What she talkin' about?"

I felt everybody was ganging up on me, including my husband. I didn't know I was crying until the tears rolled off of my face, and fell onto the table. The room was spinning and I felt at any moment, I would fall out of the chair again.

"Can you put Laila down and tell her to go into her room?" I said in a low voice as I stared Raven and Karen down.

Letting her down he instructed her to go into her room. She cried for a minute saying she wanted to go outside, and if it would be okay for her to wear the raincoat my mother bought for her. Although there wasn't an ounce of rain outside, and wearing the coat didn't make any sense, I still allowed her to do so.

When she was out of sight I said, "Raven and Karen, please leave me alone with my husband." I told them in a low but threatening tone. If either one of them would've said anything outside of okay, I would have slit both of their throats and watched them drop to the floor. Luckily for them they left without contesting.

When Hempay and I were alone, I said, "Baby, I'm sooo sorry for breaking our vows. You mean the world to me."

"Didn't I do right by you, Kiante? Didn't I give you everything you ever wanted? He asked his body shaking.

"Yes, baby." I said watching the tears fall from his face. "You made me the happiest woman in the world!"

"Then why would you crush me like this? Why, Kiante?"

"I'm a fool!" I said reaching for his hand. "And I'm sorry."

I never saw a man cry outside of the time my father did when his mother died. It was the worst moment I witnessed in all of my life. And now here I was, watching my husband cry because I disappointed him in the worst way. I never knew until this moment, how much my husband loved me and better yet, how much I loved him.

"Hempay," I said crying along with him. "Can we make this work? Can you give me the chance to show you that I love you with all of my heart? Please?"

Instead of getting an answer I got his back as he walked away.

"Hempay! Talk to me!" I sobbed. "Please!!!!"

"You said enough. It's over."

An hour later he packed his clothes and left me, while I begged with every inch of my heart.

No Amount of Help
KIANTE

My house felt so empty without my husband. It felt like and abandoned building, full of secrets and lies. As each second went by, it was apparent I couldn't live without him. I was sitting on the sofa with my daughter.

"Mommy, why can't I bite my own head?"

"Cuz you can't, baby," I sighed.

"Well, why not?"

"Because if God meant for you to bite your own head, he would've placed your teeth on top of it."

"But why, mommy?"

"Cuz, Laila," I said growing irritated at my inquisitive daughter. I was staring at the only memories of our life together on paper.

Hempay called and requested me to gather all of my bills so he could organize them with his irritating accountant. He'd been working with her for a few months and I swear I hated her guts.

He told me he was thinking about filing for divorce and didn't want to leave me stranded with all of the bills. How sweet. What about leaving me alone? After confirming with my doctor that I actually had Herpes, I knew there was no way possible he'd take me back now. And when I came home from my appointment and told him it was confirmed. He dumped me. It was nothing for him to leave everything we built together. I was trying to be calm because the doctor said getting upset would only exasperate my condition and at the rate I was going, they'd be all over my face.

"Baby, why don't you put on Dora and watch TV in your room?"

"I want to stay here with you," she whined.

"Okay but if you want to stay here with me; you'll have to be quiet."

"Who's this, mommy?" She asked going through the photo album I kept under the living room table.

"Why?" I asked noticing an old picture of me, Lucia, Marissa and J.D.

"Cause that's the man, mommy."

"What man?"

"The one who hit my face at my old school. That's him."

"What?!" I yelled. "Stop lying! You know I hate when you do that."

"It's true! He hit me, mommy."

"Laila," I said trying to prevent yelling at her. "I want you to be quiet and stop making up tales. Besides, you're in a new school so get over it."

"Mommy it's true! The man here in this picture hit me!"

"Shut the fuck up!" I screamed in her face. It was the first time I yelled at her and I felt bad instantly.

"I'm sorry, mommy."

"Don't be. Just give me a little silence."

I thought we had an understanding while we shared the living room sofa, apparently not because she was lying across my lap moving every five minutes. When I told her to stop, she started swinging her feet back and forth as she lye on her back. And every time she did, she blocked my view. All I could see was her hard plastic Bratz slippers swinging back and forth in front of me. Why couldn't she be still or play on the floor? Why did she have to be up under me? And why did she have to lie? Any other time I wouldn't mind but lately I needed space. Not to mention I needed time to go over the life me and my husband once shared on paper, while I tried to figure everything out.

When the Bratz slipper came off and knocked me in the head I was fed up. "Laila, get your ass up and go to your room! You're getting on fucking nerves!"

The look in her eyes broke my heart. Holding her heart in her hands, she still had enough love to kiss me on my cheek, and walk brokenheartedly to her room. As if I couldn't feel any lower, I felt worse.

"I'm sorry, Laila," I called out to her. "Just give me some time to be alone."

"Okay, mommy," she said disappearing to her room.

I started to make it up to her by letting her go outside and play, so she could prance around in her raincoat but the phone rang. I took my time answering it. Ever since Hempay left a month ago, I got the picture that he had no intentions of calling me. When I finally answered it, I was irritated when it was nobody but his nagging ass accountant.

"Mrs. Carey?"

"Yes." I sighed grabbing the half glass of wine on the table, fucking with this bitch; I was going to need every last bit of it.

"Hi. I'm calling to see if you've gathered the bills and your account information so that Mr. Carey can settle the accounts. He's trying to have these matters addressed as soon as possible," her voice high, her tone condescending. "Even if you didn't get the personal account information, I need the account numbers to all of your joint accounts. I have the one for Bank of America, but I need the account number you use for the business."

"I'm not helping you end my life! Tell him to get the account information himself!"

"Don't kill me, I'm just the messenger."

"Well, tell Mr. Carey that I'm doing the best I can to gather everything up for him. But I also have a business to run and I'm still raising his daughter! Alone! So please stop rushing me!"

"Ma'am," she laughed. "I'm not the one who has ended your marriage so please don't talk to me in such a malevolent tone. I'm just your husband's accountant and nothing more."

This fat bitch was pushing it. She probably had a thing for him and was trying her best to settle the bills so he wouldn't have any other reason to contact me outside of seeing his daughter. But if there was one thing I wasn't concerned about, that was Hempay wanting her. She had an overgrown mole under her nose and every time she breathed in or out the hairs on it moved. But that wasn't the worse part. Whenever she took her glasses off, her eyes met each other and she'd continue talking as if nothing was wrong.

"I'm not going to let you work my nerves, bitch! Like I said, when I get the information I will give it to you."

"You know your father, husband and friends are nothing like you. They're more professional."

"Them bitches are not my friends so don't compare me to them!"

"Mrs. Carey?!" She responded as if she was clutching her pearls. "Please don't use that type of language or tone with me or I will quit!"

The last thing I needed was her to quit. I can hear Hempay now blaming me for that too. Ever since he hired her fat ass, a month ago, she been getting on my nerves. Apparently she was so good, that my parents used her right along with Raven and Karen for their businesses.

"Like I said," I responded adding base to my voice. "The moment I gather my bills together you'll get them but not a moment sooner. I'll also make sure you get the account information, too, so tell Hempay not to worry." With that I hung up on the fat bitch's cheeks.

When it rung again I just knew she wanted some of me and I was preparing to give it to her, "HELLO!" I yelled.

"Kiante?" The voice familiar but I was so mad I couldn't make it out.

"Who's this?!"

"Raven."

You can't be serious. Did this bitch actually have the audacity to call me?! She and Karen had been calling me everyday since they ended my marriage but the calls stopped for a week. I thought they had finally gotten the message.

"Why are you calling me?!" I questioned giving her more than I should have.

"Please, Kiante. We need to talk."

"Raven, you've taken everything from me already!"

"I'm calling you to apologize," she said as if she was really concerned. "I didn't know Hempay would leave you. We just wanted you to be honest with him."

"I'm not trying to hear this shit, Raven."

"There's more. You have to be careful with the accountant your father recommended. I think something's up with her."

"You're telling me something I already know."

"We had to fire her because…"

"Raven! I don't want to hear anything you have to say," I responded cutting her off. I knew she was getting ready to lie to me and I didn't want anything she said filling my head.

"Kiante," she continued crying. "I'm trying to warn you that…"

"Did you hear what I said?!" I yelled.

"Yes!"

"Well then there's nothing left to talk about."

"Kiante," she said as if she was trying her hardest to get through to me. "You're still my best friend even if I'm not yours. Can we get past this and make things right?" Please. I miss talking to you and Karen does too."

Click!

I don't have time for the games or for talking to that fake bitch on the phone. As I went over my bills, I ran across some old account records in a manila folder held together with a rubber band. It was torn on the edges and based on where it was; I think I wasn't supposed to find it. I thought he took all of his account information and records with him, he must've forgotten about this.

I didn't handle any of the banking; he did everything with the exception of my Starbucks and personal accounts. Sitting on the couch, I went over each line item to be sure I added all my bills to the list. I hated taking care of our joint expenses. When I saw Lucia Alverez's name on several of the *automatic* transfer's lines of our banking account statement, I almost passed out. The record I was looking at dated back to December of 2001 and another I was looking at was dated for April of 2004 which meant even if the transfers had now stopped, they'd gone on far too long.

Instead of calling him, I decided to call Lucia instead. I wanted to know what connection she had with my husband behind my back.

"Kiante!" Maria said. "I haven't heard from chu since forever. How is everything with your father, Raven and Karen?"

That was weird that she asked about Raven and Karen but I left it alone.

"Everything's fine, Maria," I said not feeling up for the pleasantries. "Thanks for asking."

"No problem, sweetheart. I'm just so sorry to hear about chu and Hempay," she continued in an apologetic tone. "But I don't want you to worry, he's a good man. He'll come around."

What the fuck is going on in my life?! How did she know when I hadn't even talked to this woman since Marissa died?

"Thanks," I said sounding as if I appreciated her words. "Is Lucia in?"

"Sure," she said her voice saddened. "Che's always here."

"Well I want to speak to her for a second."

"No problem," she responded. "And Kiante, I want you to remember that whatever happens, you have each other."

"I know, Maria," I said rolling my eyes.

"Good, sweetheart. I been thinking about you a lot lately. And I'm sorry, in advance. For everything."

"That's fine, Maria! Now can I please speak to Lucia?"

"Sure. I'll go get her."

Maria was getting on my damn nerves! I don't know what her story was but I didn't have time to hear it either. Within a minute Lucia answered the phone. Her voice more upbeat and confident than it had been in the past. I figured that maybe she actually had gotten use to her physical condition after all. She needed to, considering she'd be stuck with it.

"Yes?" she said waiting for me to speak first.

"Hi, Lucia," I said hesitating. "How are you doing?"

"Yes?" She said again as if she didn't hear my question.

"I said how are you doing?" I repeated.

"If you want to play games call your friends," she said. "I'm not interested in bullshitting with you, Kiante. Now for the last time, what do you want?"

"*Okay*," I said. "Well maybe you can start by telling me why your name appears on my account records for over two thousand dollars a month."

"I could tell you," she laughed. "But I'm not going to. It isn't my place."

"Why not?!"

"Because you need to be taking your questions up with your husband, Kiante. Hempay and I have an understanding that goes beyond you. I thought you realized that when you stole him from me."

"I didn't steal anybody!" I informed her. "He walked away from you on his own."

"Apparently he didn't walk too far," she laughed. "And to think, despite my face he still has me in his heart. Humph," she sighed. "Maybe love is blind."

"Why are you trying to steal my husband?!" I asked in a jealous rage.

"Is that what you think, precious?" She said in a fake caring tone. "Because if you think that, you're terribly wrong. You get only what you deserve."

"Fuck you, Lucia!"

She started laughing and said, "Tell me something, Kiante. Was it necessary to let him bust off in your face? In the bathroom? On a toilet?"

"What are you running your half burnt lips about now?"

"I hear you have a sore on your mouth the size of Texas."

"And where did you hear that bullshit?"

"Your little friends stay coming back over here blowing up your business. Tell me something else; did he look like what your fake Blaze looked like in your mind? I mean, was that how you imagined he would look?"

"So you did have something to do with that Martin guy approaching me?"

"Hmmmm," she yawned. "I may have set up the approach, but if you really loved Hempay, you could've walked away. But you didn't. So you tell me, did you get what you deserved?"

"I hate you!" I yelled my voice flying into the receiver and hitting me back in my ear.

"After all I been through, do you really think that bothers me?" She laughed.

"Why are you doing this to me?"

"You'll find out, in time." Lucia responded. "And I might as well tell you something Karen and Raven won't."

"And what's that?"

"The fact that it was because of them that me and Hempay broke up when we were in school.

You thought he wasn't feeling me and I wasn't feeling him before the accident. In actuality, I caught the three of them fucking on the mats in school. So if you have them around Hempay now, chances are they're still doing all that and then some to him right now."

"Yeah right!" I said hoping she wasn't serious. It didn't add up. Hempay couldn't stand them and it was me constantly trying to bring them closer. But still, what if she was telling the truth. It would mean Hempay lied to me about something too. He wasn't as innocent as I thought he was.

"*Awww*....you didn't know did you?" she questioned. "Well trust me, it is true. I'm doing you a favor, and for what? Maybe I'm still a sweet person at heart. Or...maybe I wanted you to feel the same way I have been feeling. Fucked up!"

"Marissa said you broke up with him because of me."

"No," she laughed. "I didn't know he was feeling you until he got into his feelings about your so-called boyfriend Blaze. Hmmm," she said as if she remembered something. "Before that, you wasn't even in the picture."

"I hate you!" I cried.

"I know, precious," she cooed. "I know. But when your life is over. I mean, completely over, remember that it was you who started this first. I know you had something to do with my life being taken from me, and I'm not going to stop until I steal yours. Enjoy the rest of what you have left."

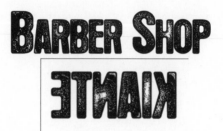

I threw on my white Rasta striped hoodie and cropped pants set by Gwen Stafani, with my white pumps. Even though I was stepping into his place of business beefing, I wanted to look cute when I confronted him. Before making a move, I needed to be certain that one of the things I approached him about was true. I knew Lucia was jealous of our relationship, so it was a great possibility that she was lying on him by saying he fucked Raven and Karen. So I decided to call Raven last week. She was so excited to hear from me that she told me exactly what I wanted to know.

"Why didn't you tell me, Raven?" I asked on my cell phone driving home from work.

"Tell you what?"

"That you and Karen slept with Hempay." I said sounding as if I was more concerned than I was mad.

"Because it happened when we were in high school." She was scared shitless and she needed to be. "We were kids. It ain't mean shit."

"So you would ruin my marriage and stand up in my house like you were so holy when for real, you and that bitch fucked my man? I'm telling you right now, had I known that, both of you bitches would've left a different way. And it damn sure would not have been walking!"

"Like I said, it wasn't even like that. We were dumb ass kids." She pleaded. "It happened one time."

"I don't' care! You were supposed to be my friend and you didn't tell me. Now I see why you kept challenging me on Hempay not being perfect. You knew first hand you scandalous ass, bitch!"

"I'm sorry, Kiante. Let's put this behind us and move on. We're like sisters."

"Bitch, we ain't hardly related. You and that other bitch ain't nothin' but two back-stabbing hoes!"

"Kiante, please," she said. "You don't mean that."

"OH but I do! I'ma tell you what it's like, the next time I see you, I'm snatching that tired ass bun out of your head. Believe that!"

With that confirmed, I called Hempay everyday asking him to call me about the accounts and our marriage but he never returned my calls. I started to tell him that something was wrong with Laila, because I knew he would answer the phone then, but we swore we'd never to play when it came to the welfare of our child, and if nothing else I wanted to respect that.

But it hurt me that he hadn't been answering or returning any of my calls. So if he wanted our business at his barbershop in front of all of his business associates and friends, I was gonna give it to him.

Before leaving the house to go to the shop, I attempted to call him. But when I picked up the phone to place a call, we didn't have a dial tone. In the past it was because Laila had knocked the Bratz phone off the hook in her room. I was almost certain that this was now the case.

"Laila!" I yelled as I put my purse on the table by the door along with my keys.

"Yes, mommy," she said running out swinging a fake sword that lit up with every move.

"Is your phone off the hook?"

"No," she whined.

"Well go make sure. I can't make a call."

"Okay, mommy," she sang running back toward her room.

While Laila checked on that, I talked to Sarah and told her we'd be home later and what to prepare for dinner. Wishfully, I told her to make enough for three. I had plans to try and get Hempay to come back with me. But when I approached her, for the first time ever, she gave me attitude right off the break. And let me tell you something, Sarah is the most passive person you'd ever meet in your life. You can knock this woman upside the head and she'd still smile and show up for work the next day. So when she acted like this, I was sure something was wrong.

"Sarah, are you okay?"

"I'm fine," her white face turning a beet red.

"Sarah, be honest with me. Is something wrong with your family?"

"Not really," she said handing my coffee to me in my favorite red cup.

"Well, what is it?"

"I haven't gotten my paycheck this week."

"I'm sorry," I smiled. "With everything that's going on, I could've sworn that I wrote you a check. It's not a problem," I said walking toward my purse. "I can write you another one right now," I continued picking up my purse to grab the checkbook.

She followed me and said, "If you don't mind, Mrs. Carey, I'd prefer cash."

"You know we prefer to write checks, Sarah. This way we can have record of payment."

"I know," she smiled. "And usually I wouldn't have a problem with it. But the last check you gave me bounced."

"What?!" I asked as if I heard her incorrectly. We had over $20,000 at any given time in our account so there was no way it could have bounced. A check from the Carey account was as good as a cashier's check. "I think you are mistaken."

"No ma'am," she said digging in her bra and handing me back the bounced check with the letters

NSF stamped on it. "It didn't go through. I was charged a fee by my bank and everything. So if you don't mind, I'd prefer cash."

I was so embarrassed! It was bad enough that she knew my husband left me, but now she was holding a bounced check in her hands. Had I done something wrong with balancing our bills? I was humiliated. And then I figured he already gotten a separate account and left me with nothing. Digging in my purse, I handed her $800. That covered her monthly fee and a little extra for the bounced check. It was all of my pocket change but I needed her to know things were still good with me, even if I was alone. Now I needed to go to the barbershop more than ever.

"I'm sorry, Sarah."

"No problem," she smiled. She was just happy to have her money and I can't say that I blamed her.

"If you can prepare the Chicken Parmesan, I'd appreciate it."

"Still make enough for three?" She confirmed sensing after Hempay heard what I had to say, he probably wouldn't be returning back with me.

"Yes. Enough for three."

I really had to talk to Hempay now. When I picked up the phone again it still wasn't on the hook. What the fuck was going on around here?!

"Laila!" I yelled walking toward her room.

REVERSED

"Yes, mommy," she said as her body shook due to being afraid of the tone in my voice. Lately I'd been very grumpy and mean.

"I thought I told you to hang up the phone?!"

"It is," she said as tears welled in her eyes. When I picked up the phone she was right, it was on the receiver. What the fuck was going on now?!!

ON MY WAY
KIANTE

With Laila strapped up in her car seat, we hit it to his barber shop in DC off of U Street N.W. His shops were all called *La-Kian's* Barbershop. He named them after me and his daughter. I plugged her IPOD into the car and let the sounds of JoJo keep her busy. Normally I was tired of hearing her sing but today, I appreciated her voice and the attention Laila gave to her.

When I pulled up into the barbershop parking lot, I cut on my phone and noticed I had 12 missed calls and 8 messages. I decided to retrieve them later because there was nothing more important to me than getting my family back. I also wanted some answers to a lot of the things I just found out.

The moment I walked in all of the talking ceased and all eyes were on me. I didn't know how much they knew and it was killing the hell out of me that they possibly knew I was unfaithful to my husband. If they were in his ear, I knew it would be hard getting him back. Niggas pride themselves on keeping other people down just cause they didn't have anybody who loved them. I couldn't see my husband on some bitch teeth shit like that, by telling them what I'd done, but couldn't be sure.

"Daddy!" Laila yelled running into her his arms the moment she saw his face.

"Hey, baby," he said taking time from his client to give his daughter a serious hug. "How's daddy's little girl?" His eyes alternated from her to me several times. I noticed how when he looked at her, there was love, but when he glanced at me, there was still hate and my heart broke inside.

"Good! The phone is off and mommy thought it was me but the dial tone not work and I listened to JoJo the whole way here." She rambled in less than 10 seconds.

Laila told him in a few seconds what most people needed one hour to say. I'm gonna have to work on her mouth because sooner or later it's going to get everybody into trouble. Walking over to Hempay I saw no signs of him missing me. He was clean shaven. His braids were fresh. He had on new kicks and new clothes. I also saw a card on his counter that I was sure came from a female. My heart sank as I tried to steal peeks at what was on it.

"What's up, Kiante?"

"Huh?"

"I said what are you doing here? What you want?" He looked like he wanted to spit in my face. "I'm working and don't need all this shit."

"So what? I can't bring your daughter here to see you?"

"It ain't my week. Now are you gonna stop playing games with me or what?" He asked while he continued to cut his client's hair as Laila ran buck wild in his shop.

"I think we should do this in private." I warned. "Everything is not for everybody."

"Listen," he said like talking to him was out of the question. "I ain't got shit to talk to you about. If it's that important it can wait until we have some privacy. Now get the fuck out of my shop."

"You got a problem?" I asked his client who was staring in my face.

Silence.

"Listen," he said mad at how I talked to his client. "Don't be comin' in here startin' no bullshit in my establishment."

"Well don't forget, nigga, that it was because of me you got this shit! I have just as much right to be in here as you. Now I'm tryin' to talk to you like an adult."

"Like I said," he responded. "We'll talk later."

"Okay," I said with my hands on my hips. "If you want to do this right here we can. Why didn't you tell me you fucked Raven and Karen? I got them bitches in my house and I'm finding out the entire time you fucked both of them. They were my fucking friends! And you fucked both of them!

Yet you tried to treat me like you was perfect. At least I ain't fuck somebody you know!"

"Dirty," Hempay yelled to another barber while grabbing me by the upper arm. "Finish dude off for me. Don't worry main man, he's good."

"He betta be," the dude grunted.

Taking me into the back of the shop, I was happy that Laila came with us on her own instead of me having to find her. All eyes were still fixed on us until we were out of sight, and the moment we were, I heard conversations resume as normal. I wasn't sure but I had an idea I'd be the talk of the shop for days to come.

"What you doing here?!" He yelled as Laila roamed around his office as if she knew *exactly* where she was going and what she was looking for. I guess she would considering he had her here on several occasions. When she located a portable game, she was in heaven. And most importantly, out of tune with us.

"Why didn't you tell me you slept with Raven and Karen? That should've been something you told me before we were married."

"Because it wasn't that serious. We were just kids."

"I'm tired of hearing that shit! You were a kid but you a man now and you should've told me that you fucked my friends."

"Well I told you they weren't your friends but you didn't listen to me."

"Yeah, but you didn't tell me why."

When he wiped his mouth as if he didn't know where to start, I was instantly moved to tears when I noticed he wasn't wearing his ring. Why did he take it off? We were still a couple, a married one at that. I loved Hempay more than anything and I decided that no matter what, I was going to be a better person. I needed to, if for nobody else, for me, and hopefully my family. But if God was listening, I really wanted my husband back.

"Hempay," I said my voice cracking. "Where is your wedding ring?"

"I don't wear it no more!"

"Why, Hempay? We're still married!"

"Yeah, but that'll be changing soon."

"What are you saying?"

"You heard me."

"Please don't leave me, Hempay. I love you. I'm so sorry for everything I've done."

"Kiante," He said taking a deep breath. "I hadn't expected you to come up here, but since you did, you might as well know that we're seriously over. I'm sorry, but you violated our marriage in a way I can't forgive. You let somebody have what's mine and that will always be on my mind."

As I looked at him I imagined how good he smelled and all I wanted him to do was hold me in his arms. I would kill for one touch from my husband. He looked so handsome in his open barber jacket, wifebeater, jeans, Timbs and fresh braids.

"If you don't want me, I guess that's something I have to deal with. But you should know I'm not going to stop trying to get you back."

"That's on you, Kiante."

"Can you tell me something though? Why would you close the accounts?"

"What you talking about?!" He asked as if he was just as shocked as I was. "I didn't fuck wit' them accounts."

"Well something's going on."

"You still got my seed in that house. As long as she's there, them accounts won't be fucked wit'. You know me better than that."

"Well, Sarah's check bounced. Now that account had over twenty G's in it. I didn't fuck with that money so something's up. I saw the bounced check and everything, here it is," I continued handing it to him to observe.

"That's some bullshit!" He yelled. "I just put 8 G's in that account yesterday."

"Well it bounced, Hempay. Plus the phone in the house is off. Even though I'm not tripping off the house phone because I use my cell, it's linked to the security system."

"Hold up," he said turning around to grab the phone. As he dialed some numbers rapidly, he repeated the same technique several times, only to do it again.

"What's wrong, Hempay?"

He threw his hand up for me to be silent.

"I know mothafuckin' well this bitch ain't get her number changed and didn't tell me!" He yelled as he stood up. "She was supposed to pay all them bills."

"Who?"

"Joan."

"She called a couple of weeks back to get my bank account information for the house and the bill information. So I know she had it."

"Hempay," a barber yelled. "Your father-in-law is out here."

"What?!" I thought out loud as I ran to the door. I wondered what daddy would be doing here especially since he knew we weren't together. The moment I saw his face and the fright upon it, I knew something was terribly wrong.

"What's up, pops?" Hempay asked.

"Everything's gone man. She took everything." His voice quick and broken.

"Who, daddy?" I asked noticing he looked like he was about to pass out.

"The accountant," he said holding his chest. "She took everything! My life savings is all gone!"

"I don't understand," I continued as Hempay ran by his side to support him from falling.

"Awww!" he yelled as he balled over in pain and fell on the ground of the barber shop holding his chest.

"Daddy! Daddy! What's wrong?! What's wrong!!!?"

FROM BAD TO WORSE

I saw them in my rearview mirror but I had no intentions on stopping. Hempay called me to tell me that my father's condition was worsening so I had to leave the baby with Sarah to go see about him. I grabbed the mail and noticed a letter was in it with J.D's name. I knew Hempay didn't like him just as much as J.D. hated him so it was odd that he would write to him. It also reminded me that I never told him that Laila had pointed to him as the one who slapped her all of those times at school.

The moment I pulled out of my driveway, I could see the headlights of Raven's gold Mercedes Benz still following me. When I glanced at the passenger seat, Karen was right next to her.

On cue Raven's mobile phone number appeared on the display of my car phone. I wished both of these bitches would leave me alone. After everything was confirmed that they slept with my husband, I felt stupid for having them around me and my family.

I found a parking lot in the garage of Washington Hospital Center and ran inside. I was so out of it that I left my purse. I only hoped nobody would get any ideas and break my car window, before I had a chance to pick it up.

"I'm here to see Mr. Jenkins. I'm his daughter," I advised the lady at the front desk.

"Do you know what room he's in?"

"No, I think he was moved to intensive care. And can you hurry up a little? I don't want him to die because I'm out here waiting on you."

"Ma'am you have to be patient. I'm checking on it now."

As I waited on this bitch to tell me where my father was, I glanced at the Rolex on my arm and figured only twenty minutes passed since Hempay called and told me things were worse. As if I hadn't been through enough, Raven and Karen trotted their asses right up to the counter where I stood.

"We need to talk to you," Raven said.

"For what?" I asked hoping the woman would give me the information I needed to leave these two bitches standing alone. "I don't have shit to say to ya'll. I told you that over the phone."

"Well you have to make time," Karen added.

"How you sound? The only thing I have to make time for is for you to get the fuck out of my face."

"He's in ICU on the third floor," the front desk woman said. "You can take the elevator to the second, and take the stairs up to the third. For some reason it's not working properly."

When she gave me the information I needed, I hurried to the elevator which appeared to open for me the moment I stepped to it. And instead of Raven and Karen going home, they walked right in. It was then that I noticed how they were dressed. Raven had on a white wife beater, army fatigues and timbs. Karen had on a sweat suit and tennis shoes. If you knew them you'd know this was totally out of the ordinary.

When the elevator door opened on the 2nd floor, I walked out and again they followed me. There was no way I was carrying that bullshit to my father's room so I decided to hear what the fuck they had to say.

"What?!"

"You owe us some money," Raven said.

"Bitch, what are you talking about now?"

"You heard what the fuck I said! Hempay's accountant drained our accounts and it's all your fault."

"Hold up," I said laughing at the idea of paying them anything. "I didn't tell you to use anybody. You wanted to know who Hempay was using and I told you he found somebody new. It's not my fault your old accountant left and you had to find another one."

"Bitch, it is all your fault!" Karen yelled approaching me. "And I want my money."

I knew then that they were serious. As I glanced down the hall I noticed that it appeared vacant. There was a yellow sign on the floor that indicated that it had been recently mopped. A flood of fear took over me because I knew I had to fight. Now defending myself wasn't the problem, but losing my father while I was in the process of fighting was.

"Listen," I said waving them off. "We'll discuss this shit later. Right now, I have more important things to worry about."

The moment I said that Karen hit me upside my head with what felt like a bat. I fell up against a hospital room door, forcing it open with my weight. Moments later, Raven came over top of me and started stomping me with the timbs she was wearing. Desperately trying to recuperate from the initial blow, I lay there on the floor like a punching bag while they kicked me over and over again. This wasn't supposed to be like this. If anything, they should be kissing my ass.

"What's going on?" I heard an older male voice say.

I hadn't even realized that we weren't alone in the partially dark room.

"I said what's going on?" He repeated.

His question gave me time to pull myself together. When I saw what looked like piss next to his bed, I decided to go for it. They didn't see it

REVERSED

coming when I threw all of it in their faces getting a little on my hands.

"Ugggghhh! That bitch threw piss in my face!" Raven yelled tearing off her clothes to get some of it off.

"I'm gonna really kick your ass now," Karen responded doing the same.

As they messed with their piss drench clothes, I ran to the elevator and went to the fourth floor. With my father still on my mind, I only hoped that I'd be able to see him before something fatal happened. When I hobbled off of the elevator and pulled my weight down the steps to the third floor, I smiled when I saw my husband right by his bedside. Considering what just happened, it made everything seem a little better. For now anyway.

Not My Daddy
KIANTE

"Daddy," I sniffled trying to avoid from crying. "Remember when I was little and you use to tell me that no matter what, I can always count on you? Well," I paused wiping the tears from my eyes. "I'm gonna need you to make good on your promise daddy. Because…if…if you leave me, I don't know what I'm gonna do. I don't think I can make it without you." As I broke down, I looked at my father's hands, they were the same hands that always held me and made me feel as if everything was okay. It killed me to think that there was a possibility that I'd never be held by him again.

Once the realization of losing him set in I was no more good. I broke down so hard, that my husband had to lift my body off my father's. How could this happen to a man who doesn't deserve it?! I had so much anger toward the so-called accountant that I didn't know what to do. Although this was something I couldn't have foreseen, I still felt responsible.

Before I met Hempay, Daddy was the number one man in my life. And even if Hempay left me, I took comfort in knowing that he would always be there and now there was a great possibility that this would no longer be true.

My mother had already been taken out and placed in a hospital bed of her own because every time she came in the room to see him, she'd pass back out. Daddy wasn't just a father; he was the epitome of all that was great and good.

"Baby," Hempay said hugging me in his strong arms to comfort me. "Everything's gonna be okay. Come sit down over here."

As my legs gave out several times on the way to the seat next to my father's bed, I desperately tried to comply and believe what he was saying was true. But the doctors already told us what to expect, and their diagnosis wasn't good. Even Laila was devastated at what was happening. She couldn't understand why her grandpoppy was sprawled out on the floor of her daddy's barber shop. And as if I was four years old myself, I wouldn't understand either.

"Baby," Hempay said rubbing my legs. "You wanna tell me why you can barely walk yourself? What happened to your face and arms?"

"Not right now, Hempay. I just want to spend some time with my father."

"I understand," he said in a deep caring voice. "But if somebody hurt you, I need to know why."

"I promise I'll tell you the moment all of this is over. I just don't want to talk about this now."

"You got it," he responded backing down.

"Why this have to happen to my daddy?" I asked crying on his shoulders. "I don't understand!"

His eyes roamed toward my father as he held his head down. I knew what he was thinking. His parents have been dead a long time. They weren't dead in life, but in spirit. Like stories told in most projects, they were victims of the streets and as a result, sold their souls to it by using and abusing drugs. Hempay took to the streets to support himself while always planning to get in and get out. I like to think when he met me, that was suddenly possible.

"I don't know, baby," he said rubbing my arms as we stared at my father's bed hoping he'd wakeup. "Sometimes fucked up shit happens to the best of people. But you know what, baby," he said looking into my eyes. "I just don't see God taking him now. I don't."

"Why you say that?" I said looking into his eyes for the hope I needed to believe he had the answers.

"Cause God knows I need him just as much as you do. He's been like a father to me, Kiante. Despite what we were going through he's a good man and I need his guidance in my life too."

REVERSED

When I saw a tear fall down my husband's face, I fell in love with him all over again. I made a decision that today I was going to change my life. I didn't know how or where I would even start, but I knew I had to try. All my life my father told me to put trust in my family, God and myself. I realized that my life had been altered, but if God could see it to give me another chance, I swore I'd put everything into my marriage and family leaving all other shit by the side. All I wanted was for the three of us to remain a family and for my father to be alive. God help us. Please.

SAD DAY KIANTE

My father passed away on a Sunday, a few days ago. To tell you how I feel would be impossible, it just can't be done. He was the closet thing to perfection in my life. Me and my mother have been walking around like zombies trying to hold things together. But how can you hold things together when the foundation is missing? Hempay had been very supportive, and although he has come back home, this was not the way I imagined it would happen. I didn't want to win my husband back based on pity, but that's exactly the way I had gotten my family back.

My mother asked me to tell Mamma Maria that the funeral would be tomorrow, but when we called I was surprised to find out the home phone was disconnected. So she wouldn't have to be bothered with going over their house, me and Hempay agreed to take the ride there ourselves. To be honest I wasn't feeling the trip because I didn't feel like seeing Lucia. I was still trying to sort out my part in everything and what she did wrong. Part of me, a big part of me hated her guts.

REVERSED

We were trying to get over having to bury my father, and live on $300 dollars between us since the so called accountant stole everything we owned. She got away with $30,000 from our account and over $40,000 from daddy and mommy's. I heard she took Karen and Raven for 25 grand. I have to be honest; I wasn't too concerned with their loss considering what they did to me. And although I didn't want to tell Hempay, since he kept asking, I had to be honest about our fight at the hospital. He told me not to worry and that he would handle it. So I left it right there.

The doctor said daddy died from a heart attack, but I think he died from a broken heart. When he saw all of the money was gone, he knew the dream wedding he was preparing went out of the window with it. When mamma found out what he was doing, from reading his journal, she broke down again. Everybody was trying to pull it together. We went from riches back to rags and had lost somebody who could never be replaced. Although we stood to gain from his life insurance policy for over $100,000, it didn't replace him and it never would.

"You coming in?" Hempay asked me as we pulled up into Tyland Towers parking lot to see Mamma Maria.

"I hadn't planned on it," I said with my head hung low. "I think I'ma stay here."

"You sure?" He asked in a soft voice.

I hadn't yet expressed to him that Lucia was the one who framed me with Martin or whatever his name was. To me it wasn't important right now. But the more I thought about it, maybe it wasn't a good idea to send my husband in there alone to be subjected to more of Lucia's pity.

"I'll come with you," I regretfully said.

We parked our car in the same place we use to when we use to visit Lucia and Marissa. The car looked eerie being there, especially when there was no Marissa. And then I thought about Lucia being burned. I could even hear her screams like it happened yesterday. Once out of my car, Victor sped up next to us on his bike. He was older but still very handsome. It looked like he was twelve or thirteen and had shot up in height from when we last saw him.

"Sorry about your dad, Kiante," he said stopping on his bike in front of us.

"Thanks, Victor," I smiled, as best as I could. "I appreciate that."

"You goin' to see Maria?" He asked.

"Yeah lil man," Hempay said. "She here?"

"No, she moved. Everybody knows that," he responded with the same little boy arrogance he always had.

"Moved where?"

"I Uhn No. I just know her and J.D packed up and moved sometime last week. I seen them taking out their things and everything."

"Is Lucia still here?" Hempay continued.

"I uhn know. Ever since she sold her car, we never know if she's here or not. A lot of the kids around here are scared of her. They call her the Scar face. I tell them she use to be real pretty but they don't believe me."

"Oh," Hempay said. "Well," he said digging into his pocket. "Here you go."

"Thanks, man. I'll catch ya'll later. And start comin' around more!"

We stared at each other for a moment because I didn't hear nothing about her moving, and I knew Hempay didn't either. I was also wondering how much money he gave him because until we got back on our feet, we needed all of our money. After thinking about it for a second I realized that it was possible that someone did tell us. To be honest all I was thinking about was the loss of my father.

We knocked on the door several times. Hempay banged so hard that other people came out thinking he was knocking on their door. I heard the rain pouring down out of the sky as we waited for somebody to answer. After realizing she wasn't there, we headed back to the car. The rain drenched us as if someone had poured buckets of water over our heads. Once inside the car, we sat in silence as beads of water ran down our bodies.

"I gotta tell you something," Hempay began.

"What is it?" I was worried that he'd tell me he didn't want to be with me after all. The last thing

I needed now was my marriage ending…again. "I hope it's not anything bad because I can't take it right now."

"I know," he continued. "It's not bad but it is something you should know."

"Okay," I paused. "What is it?"

"I've been looking after Lucia for some time now."

"Looking out? What does that mean?"

"I've been putting money in her account ever since that shit happened to her. I don't know why I'm telling you except, I want to come clean with you about everything. If we're going to work."

"Well there's something I should tell you, too."

"Go ahead."

"Well," I started carefully. "Lucia was the one who sent that guy to me."

"What guy?"

"The one who gave me Herpes."

"I'm not tryin' to hear that shit!"

"It's true," I said. "I wouldn't make up shit like that. I wouldn't risk losing you again after God saw fit to bring you back to me."

"So you're telling me she intentionally set it up for you to get some shit like that?" He paused. "That don't make no fucking sense. I mean, how could she even find somebody like that?"

"I don't know. But I do know she had everything to do with how we met."

"I can't think about that right now," he advised. "It still hurts to hear how you disregarded our marriage vows."

"There's more, Hempay."

"Come on, Kiante! I woulda never started talking if I knew all of this was gonna come out again."

"I have to tell you this, baby," I continued, as the rain on the car continued to fall on the windows as we drove down the road leading closer to our house. "Remember Laila was getting slapped at school and we thought it was one of her friends."

"Yeah."

"Well before daddy died she pointed out J.D in an album. I didn't believe her then but I'm starting to believe her now. She said he was the one who hit her all those times. She pointed him out the moment she saw his face and I believed her."

"Are you telling me that this nigga laid hands on my daughter?"

"I think so."

"For what?"

"I don't know," when I said that I realized he sent him a letter. I had forgotten all about it. "Wait a minute," I said reaching in my glove compartment. "He sent you something a while back."

Hempay snatched the letter out of my hands and read it aloud.

What up Playa,

I told you I'd get you back. I have to admit, terrifying your daughter everyday at school was the highlight to my day. That's why when you came to Marissa's funeral, I got out of Dodge. I knew the moment she saw me she'd recognize me. One time I slapped her six times in a row and I loved every minute of it. To hurt something you loved after everything you did to me.

Hempay paused from reading the letter and looked up to me. His eyes were red and his face was wet with tears. I knew the thought of Laila experiencing pain on account of something he did angered him.

Right when you moved her out of the school, I started to put a bullet in her head. I went up there waiting for her to come out and soon found out she was gone. That was a smart move. But I wasn't done. I had to see to it that you get fully what you deserved. So I sent my boy to a party your wife had one night. He told me she went on and on about how much money you and her pops had. So we sent his wife to pose as an accountant. Thanks for giving us Raven and Karen because that was an added bonus. If you're wondering was your precious Mamma Maria in on it I'd have to say yes. But don't be mad at Maria, she does whatever I say. She's supposed to. Well enjoy the rest of your life.

Lada
J.D

REVERSED

Hempay balled the letter up and slammed his fist down on my dashboard cracking it slightly. I was too afraid to think about what had been happening to Laila. I mean, did he do more than just slap her?

When we made it to the house I parked unevenly and he finally spoke.

"I'll see you in the house," he said getting out and slamming the door behind him.

As I watched him walk halfway up the driveway I thought about everything. It seemed like I couldn't get a break. Shit went from worse to shit in seconds flat. First I get herpes, than I'm ousted by my fake best friends, then I lose my husband, then my father and now I'm probably losing my husband again. I can't catch a break.

I was about to do a better job of parking when I remembered I needed to collect the deposits from my store. After that fraud stole our money, I decided to be hands on with everything until we got back on our feet. Things were tight enough as it was with money and I couldn't afford to lose one red penny. I needed everything to add up.

When I reached my business, my employees had tons of cards for me regarding the loss of my father. And although I was thankful, there was no amount of condolences that could make me feel any better. Instead of being rude, I passed out several thank you's and went on my way after collecting the money from the store.

On the way home, I played *Tru Love* by Faith Evans at least six times. This song represented how I felt about Hempay. He was everything to me and I regretted letting a cheap moment come in between that. If we could just get past everything, I swore to put all of my time and energy into my family.

When I glanced down at my ringing car phone I saw it was my mother's number. I didn't want to be depressed but I thought about how I'd feel if I had lost my husband. I would want someone to talk to also.

"Hey, mamma. Is everything okay?"

"Yeah, baby. I'm making it. How are you doing?"

"So so…," I advised. "I'm just worried about you. Have you eaten anything since the last time I saw you?"

"A little."

"You really should eat more, ma."

"I know, baby. I'll try."

"Mamma, please remember that you have the keys to my home. If you want to come early you can. We'd love to have you. You don't have to be alone."

"I know, baby."

"I love you, mamma."

"I love you too.

My mother was getting better in that now she was moving around. Before that, she wouldn't

get out of bed and stopped going to work. Hempay
and I offered to let her stay with us but she had a
major fear of guns and knew Hempay had plenty of
them lying around everywhere. But after he showed
her that they were neatly locked up and safe, and
that the key was far away from the actual weapons,
she agreed to come over more.

When I pulled up to our house, the hairs on
the back of my neck stood up when I saw my husband's truck door open. The last time that happened, he told me that Marissa died. Seeing it again
was like deja vu and I was overwhelmed with terror. I couldn't understand why his truck door was
open especially with it pouring down raining outside. And where was he going? Before I left him he
was upset and I'd just dropped him off. I couldn't
see him wanting to leave to go anywhere.

I knew that whatever was happening I'd
have to deal with it. I reluctantly parked my car and
walked up the terrifying steps toward my house.
The door opened automatically without me entering
the key, and I was scared all over again. When I
saw the face of the last person I expected to see
standing in my living room, I suddenly felt faint.

"What are you doing here, Lucia?" I asked
after looking at my husband sitting on the couch
with the gun she held in her right hand pointed
firmly toward his head.

"Why don't you sit down and I'll explain
everything to you," Lucia spat at me.

"No, I'd like to know what the fuck you're doing here!"

"And I said," she responded in a low calculating voice. "Sit the fuck down and I'll tell you everything. Don't worry, all of your questions will be answered tonight. But also…make no mistake…tonight I'm in fucking charge!"

When I walked in, I almost tripped. When I looked down to see what caught me off balance, I noticed a white cord leading from the top of the door. It was connected to a metal bucket. She must've taken some serious time to set everything up, I began to wonder what she had in store, for me and my family.

"What's that?" I asked pointing at it while I remained standing. "What's going on, Lucia?"

"Like I said," she smiled. "You're getting ready to find out."

"Where's my daughter?" I asked as my chest began to rise and fall due to crying. "Where's Laila?"

"She's outside, baby," Hempay said trying to remain calm. "Come over here and sit next to me."

"Yes," Lucia said as she placed the cigarette in the corner of her disfigured lips. "Why don't you go over there and sit next to your husband." My legs managed to walk toward him, and when I sat next to him, his arms embraced me and held me closely. Ironically it was the first real affection he'd shown me since my father died, or at least I thought so. And I took comfort in it. Obviously our show of affection angered her even more because she said, "Look at the fucking perfect family. Isn't this cute."

"What do you want, Lucia?" Hempay said growing angrier at how she was terrifying me. "My family doesn't deserve this shit! I've been good to you and we've been through enough."

"You've been good to me?" She laughed hysterically. "Is that what you call it? Good to me? You have been the worst to me of all, Hempay!"

"I've taken care of you for years! So yes, I've been good to you!"

"Well I have a different word for how you treated me. You left me when I needed you the most."

"You broke up with me! After you found out about me and your friends! You said you didn't want me anymore."

"But you didn't fight harder! You were supposed to fight for me!"

"Well, deal with me if you're mad I left you. Not my family!" Hempay yelled.

"Your family? What about me and mine?! It's because of that bitch right there," she said pushing the barrel of the gun to my cheek causing it to press up against my teeth. "That I'll never have a life again or a family of my own! So you tell me Hempay, what about me? What about everything that was taken from me?"

"Lucia, I'm sorry," he said with his hands in the air as if he was trying to plead our cases all the while praying she wouldn't pull the trigger. "But that was the past. We were kids then. It was fucked up. I know it was. But do you really want to kill anybody else tonight?"

"What?!" I yelled causing her to jump slightly as I looked around the room for my daughter. Who had died tonight already? Something told me it couldn't be Laila because the despair in his face was that of remorse but not of a father who had just lost a child. "Did she hurt Laila?!"

"Calm down, baby," he said. "Let's remain calm."

"Baby, who did she kill?!"

"Your maid!" she laughed. "How do you think I was able to rig this little concoction over your door?"

"Why!" I cried wondering what she endured before she was killed.

"Because she was in my way," she advised. "But she fought like shit! I think she thought I was trying to kill the bitch of a daughter ya'll have together, but I was like nawwww," she continued shaking her head gun pointing in our direction. "Killing her would be too easy for you two. I have something else planned for her that'll make us even."

"And what's that?" I questioned.

"You'll see in my time."

"Who does your plan involve, Lucia?" I asked as my husband listened attentively waiting on her answer.

"Don't worry," she responded trying to produce a smile on what was left of her face. "I'll get to that in a minute but first you have to tell me why you never came clean to everyone about what you did to my face?"

I figured Marissa must've confessed what we did before she killed herself. Here was my chance to admit my wrongs but suddenly I didn't want to take it. If I hadn't made a promise to my father on his deathbed to be a better person, for the sake of my family, I would've lied. Of course if I did tell her what she wanted to hear, I could make matters worse.

"What do you mean?"

"YOU KNOW WHAT THE FUCK I MEAN, KIANTE!" She yelled.

"I don't."

"YES YOU DO!! You're the one who did this to my fuckin' face, bitch!! So stop playin' games with me before I blow Hempay's face off and have you lick up the blood and guts!" She yelled cocking the gun.

"Lucia, please," Hempay begged. "Don't do this."

"Fuck you, Hempay! You can play with your wife's mind, but not with mine."

"I'm not trying to play anyone. I just want us to talk about this sensibly. Whatever involvement you think Kiante had with the condition of your face, you're wrong."

"How the fuck you know?!" She hollered. "You don't know shit!"

When she raised her voice I hoped that Laila wouldn't come out thinking I was calling her. I prayed that wherever she was, she'd stay.

"Okay, okay. I'm sorry," he said with his palms faced her direction. "I didn't mean to upset you. I just think this has gone too far. If you let us go, you don't have to worry about anybody finding out about this murder. We'll say someone tried to rob us. I know some dudes that can come in here and make all of this shit disappear. It ain't nothin' but a call, Lucia. But you gotta stop this shit now."

As scary as that sounded, I knew he was telling the truth.

"It's too late for that shit! This bitch changed all of that a long time ago. But you know what, before Marissa came to me crying about what *they'd* done, I already knew both of them had something to do with it," she continued as she walked over to me. "I felt like coming over here and putting a bullet in Kiante's face," she started laughing hysterically. "All I could do was think about what I'd do the next time I saw you. Luckily for you I figured death would be too easy, but it wasn't for my sister. She owed me more than covering up the lie you two shared. An accident or not, we were family! So I made her write a letter saying she killed herself, and when she was done, I held her down, and slit her wrists for her. I will say this, Kiante, she didn't give up much of a fight. She was ready to die. Are you?"

"You killed your own sister?" I asked.

"What do you think?"

"I don't understand why you would do that!" I screamed.

"Because she betrayed me. For you! And now you're going to pay."

"No….no…," I cried shaking my head. "Lucia, I'm so sorry. We never meant to hurt you. It was an accident! You have to believe me!"

"That's just it, it doesn't matter now. Too much time has passed and all it proved was that you were not remorseful. You stole my friends, my man and my sister. You took my life!"

"I didn't."

"Yes you did! And you held the truth from me about the accident. She told me how you tried to fuck up my car. But it didn't matter to you. You wanted my life and you took it. You're pretty fucking good."

"Well, what about everything you've taken from me? Because of what you did, my father's dead! Don't you think I've lost enough?"

"Oh….you think I had something to do with your money being stolen," she laughed. "No…I didn't do that…that was my mother and J.D. I just found that out the other day. They're probably out of the states right now. I don't know how much they took from ya'll, but it must've been enough to go away for a minute."

Me and Hempay just shook our heads. I knew J.D had everything to do with it from the expression on Hempay's face after reading the letter, but I didn't think Mamma Maria was in on it too.

"Why did J.D do this to my family?" I asked thinking had it not happened, my father would be alive today.

"Because Hempay got out on him that's why! When he kept coming to mamma's rescue in front of all of us. He didn't feel like a man and he never got over that shit. I guess everybody's lives changed for the worse huh? Six years ago I woulda never thought my mother would leave me to run off with that bum J.D! A man who came in my room every night to fuck me."

"I'm sorry he raped you, Lucia. I'm so sorry."

"What are you talking about, Kiante? J.D coming into the room to fuck me wasn't rape. I knew what I was doing. The only messed up part was he made me cut the lights out when he fucked me, but at least I got some dick. He liked having sex with the person I use to be before I was burned and couldn't bare to see the face of the new me. But that's not what this is about today now is it? This is about you, your husband, and your little girl."

"If you touch my daughter I'ma kill you!" Hempay offered.

"You can try. But I can promise you, before you even try I'll have two of these in your head."

When we saw the front door open, my heart sank. Laila was coming inside and we jumped when Lucia ran over toward the door to pull on the cord she had connected to the bucket. The moment she tugged it, some liquid fell out. When I saw the mat in front of the door began to smoke, I knew exactly what it was. My heart dropped when I saw most of it fall onto my daughters tiny body and the raincoat she was wearing.

Hempay, no longer caring about the gun in her hand, ran over to Lucia pummeling her to the floor. I immediately ran over to Laila. My breaths were rapid as I saw the raincoat she was wearing smoking. It was acid! She was trying to hurt my baby like I hurt her. I desperately began to pull the coat off of Laila as Hempay continued to fight with Lucia for the gun. My hands were burning as the acid began to eat my flesh but I didn't care. My daughter's life was on the line.

I took her toward the bathroom without regard for the pain I was in. I remembered what the doctor said when Lucia was burned that if we acted fast; a lot of the damage could be prevented. I could only imagine that the damage would've been worse if it was not for the thick raincoat my mother bought her. And to think I hated a coat that now saved her life.

Laila was screaming because her arms and legs were burning. Once inside the bathroom, I ran cold water all over her body, tearing the clothes completely off of her. My heart broke when I saw how frightened my little girl was as she held her burning arms tightly in the freezing cold water. When Laila heard Hempay and Lucia fighting in the living room, she wrapped her arms around me as the wetness from her body pressed against me and my skin.

"Who is that lady, mommy?" She asked. "Why does she want to hurt me?"

"She's somebody who's mad at me and daddy. But everything will be okay, baby. Do you believe me?"

She nodded her head yes. Examining her body I could see the damage was minimal. Just a few small burns on her arms and forehead. She had gotten away with her life and beauty.

"Now listen, Laila," I said holding the sides of her face, wiping the water out of her eyes while I looked into them. "Mommy needs you to be a big girl and stay in here. And don't open the door until you're sure it's my voice."

"Why, mommy?!" She cried shaking her head no. "Please don't leave me."

"Listen, Laila," I said trying to speak to her calmly while firmly. "I need you to be a big girl and stop crying. Can you do that for mommy?"

"Yes," she said nodding her head up and down. When I noticed she was shaking from fear and from being cold, I took her out the water and wrapped a big towel around her body.

"Now what do I want you to do?"

"Stay in here."

"And what else?"

"Not move until I hear your voice."

"Good girl," I said kissing her on the forehead.

"Ow. That burns!" She said when I kissed her head.

"I'm sorry, baby. I'll be right back." I said standing up.

"You promise?" She asked looking up at me.

"Yes, baby. I promise."

When I walked out of the door, I closed it and said a silent prayer hoping I wouldn't break the promise I just made to her. When I went into the living room, I didn't see Lucia or Hempay anywhere. What I heard next made me pee on myself. I heard my husband yell, moments before the sound of a bullet rang out. She did it! She actually shot Hempay.

Running toward the sound, I tried desperately to fight the sensation that fear was placing on me because it was hindering my movement. When I finally made it to the basement, I didn't see Lucia anywhere. What I did see was my husband's arm with his wedding ring outstretched as he lay on his side.

Running over to him I cried heavily as if that would bring him back. Over and over an eerie thought ran in my head that this was all my fault. When I noticed a lot of blood was escaping his body, I grabbed a towel we used for the bar and a five pound weight and put it on the womb. I was trying to prevent as much blood from escaping as possible. I was sure I lost him and that I'd never hear him tell me he loved me again.

"Nooooooooo!!!!! God, Noooooo!!!!" I was so caught up in grief for myself that I forgot that Laila was all alone in the bathroom waiting on my return.

I ran toward her although it felt as if my legs were made of Jell-O. I fell halfway down the hall when I heard a bullet ring out again.

"LAILA! LAILA!"

I was overwhelmed with nausea at the idea that in that bathroom, my daughter was possibly dead. When I opened the door she was still there.

"Mommy! I'm scared."

"Stay in here, Laila! And lock the door!" I advised her.

I couldn't believe I left it unlocked when I first left her. Before leaving, I tugged on it and made sure it was locked. I crept softly in the living room and still I saw nothing. It was obvious she shot at someone. With any luck, it would be herself she killed. When I reached the swinging door leading to the kitchen I pushed it open carefully. There on the floor I saw Lucia fighting for breath. She did shoot herself! I thought.

I pushed my way in and got a glimpse of what was really going on.

"Mamma?" I said watching her hold a shaking gun in her hand.

"Yes," she said as the gun was still pointed in the direction of Lucia's limp body.

"What are you doing?"

"She tried to take the rest of my life from me. I couldn't see that happening." She paused. "I'm not going to lose another person in my family. I just can't!"

"How long have you been here?"

"I've been here the entire time. Just couldn't find the best time to help you all."

"You heard everything, mamma?"

"Yes, baby," she said sobbing. "I did. And don't you worry none about that. We all make mistakes. And you made a few."

Seeing her uneasiness with weapons I knew I had to take the gun from her before she shot something else by mistake.

"Let me take this from you, mamma," I said softly as I approached her. The weapon was shaking and I feared at any moment it would go off again. When I finally got it from her clutches, she cried in my arms.

"Go call 911, mamma. Hempay needs an ambulance," I paused. "I'm going to look after Lucia."

"Okay, baby. I had to do it right? I had to shoot her to save my family."

"Yes, you did." I assured her. "And that's gonna be exactly what I tell the police."

When my mother was out of sight, I got on my hands and knees and hovered over Lucia's body. Her eyes were meeting mine and I could tell she was scared.

"Lucia," I said grabbing one of her bloody hands. "Can you hear me?"

She nodded her head yes. I got in her ear and said, "The night of the accident, do you remember me rushing into the living room to tell you that someone was messing with your car?"

She nodded her head yes.

"I did that so that you could walk outside to check on it. Do you understand what I'm saying, Lucia?"

She shook her head no.

"I'm telling you, that I knew exactly what I was doing. I meant to burn you, bitch. Not your car. Goodbye."

After I revealed my secret, I took my hands and smothered her face. When her breaths were completely gone, I stood up and brushed myself off. If my husband had died, there was no way on earth she'd be still alive, even in a jail cell. I would probably have paid someone to kill her for me.

I know it was fucked up, that I burnt this bitch on purpose, but she had what I wanted and I would do whatever I could to take Hempay from her. To be honest, it felt good getting rid of my secret because finally, I can move on. With my life. And my family.

New Life

The wind was perfect as we sat on the grass. It was Father's Day and like old times we were sharing it with him in spirit. My mother packed sandwiches, fruit, juices and snacks. It had been a tradition to share Father's Day with daddy and whether he was with us or not, we were not going to change it.

"You okay, baby?" My mamma asked as I lie on my back next to my father's tomb rubbing my 8-month-old pregnant belly.

"Yeah," I smiled looking at the sunny sky. "I'm okay. I miss him though."

"Me too," she responded lying right next to me. "But if I know your father he's here right now looking at us."

We were contemplating on life when Laila walked up and kissed both of us on the cheeks. She had one scar remaining over her left eye from that night. Other than that, she didn't show any signs of remembering what happened to her. My mom told

282

me I might have to get her help, but until she showed she needed it, I didn't want to remind her of such an awful night.

"Hey, you," my mother said tickling her. "What you doing kissing me?"

Laila was laughing so hard she couldn't answer.

"You want another sandwich, baby?" Hempay asked me. "I'm gonna get me another."

"No I'm good, honey."

"You know I love you, Kiante?" He asked as my mother smiled at both of us. "And that you mean so much to me."

"I know. And I love you, too."

Hempay was fine too after that night despite having to walk with a limp. Luckily for him the bullet entered and left him causing minor damage. We hated talking about how things had changed ever since our problems with the Alverez family. The messed up part about it was, had they not come into our lives, we would not have been together. After all, I met him through the Alverez's.

The part Hempay regretted the most that night was not being able to defend Laila. He didn't think I knew, but I had an idea that he was still looking for J.D and Mamma Maria. For me things were simple, in order to move on, I had to let go of the past and that life. So I did. Lucia was dead, Marissa was gone and J.D and Mamma Maria had run away. It was truly time to let go.

Karen and Raven lost their businesses and shortly after that, both of their houses burned down and everything in them. Since they were too ghetto to get insurance on their 500 thousand dollar homes, they lost all of their belongings. The clothes, the jewelry and the cash they kept in safes were all lost. Needless to say after that both of their husbands wanted a divorce. The businesses couldn't withstand the loss they took financially so I hear they're back to their usual games by tricking dudes and getting paid, to keep some resemblance of the lives they use to lead. I personally never talked to either of them bitches again.

I asked Hempay did he have anything to do with their homes burning down and he said, "What goes around comes around." I knew immediately he did. He probably did it after I told him how they beat me the day I visited my father in the hospital.

That saying holds a lot of meaning for me. What goes around does come around. It's true. What you put out in the world will come back to you. With that said, I'm one of the few people who believes that you can control the way if flows back to you to some extent. Because when it came around to me, I put it in Reverse.

CARTEL PUBLICATIONS
PRESENTS

The Cartel Collection
Established in January 2008
We're growing stronger by the month!!!
www.thecartelpublications.com

Cartel Publications Order Form
Inmates ONLY get novels for $10.00 per book!

Titles		*Fee*
Shyt List	_____	$15.00
Shyt List 2	_____	$15.00
Pitbulls In A Skirt	_____	$15.00
Pitbulls In A Skirt 2	_____	$15.00
Pitbulls In A Skirt 3	_____	$15.00
Victoria's Secret	_____	$15.00
Poison	_____	$15.00
Poison 2	_____	$15.00
Hell Razor Honeys	_____	$15.00
Hell Razor Honeys 2	_____	$15.00
A Hustler's Son 2	_____	$15.00
Black And Ugly As Ever	_____	$15.00
Year of The Crack Mom	_____	$15.00
The Face That Launched a Thousand Bullets		
	_____	$15.00
The Unusual Suspects	_____	$15.00
Miss Wayne & The Queens of DC		
	_____	$15.00
Year of The Crack Mom	_____	$15.00
Familia Divided	_____	$15.00
Shyt List III	_____	$15.00
Shyt List IV	_____	$15.00
Raunchy	_____	$15.00
Reversed	_____	$15.00

Please add $4.00 per book for shipping and handling.
The Cartel Publications * P.O. Box 486 * Owings Mills * MD * 21117

Name: _____

Address:_____

City/State:_____

Contact # & Email:_____

Please allow 5-7 business days for delivery. The Cartel is not
responsible for prison orders rejected.